# Good Benito

**Also by Alan Lightman**

*Einstein's Dreams*

# Good Benito

### Alan Lightman

PANTHEON BOOKS
NEW YORK

Library of Congress Cataloging-in-Publication Data
Lightman, Alan P., 1948–
Good Benito / Alan Lightman.
p.    cm.
ISBN 0-679-43614-6
I. Title.
PS3562.I45397G66    1995
813'.54—dc20                94-25957

Book Design by Fearn Cutler
Manufactured in the United States of America

This book is dedicated to my parents

# Good Benito

**H**e stands up from the boxes and looks out the window. To the east, in the distance, rises the steeple of a chapel, fragile and faint. The light changes. A cloud drifts over the sun. Then the sun is uncovered again, the little room fills up with light.

He lets down the blinds but keeps the slats open. Strips of light slide from the wall to the floor. He returns to his boxes, unpacks. A set of keys. A faded photograph of a young woman with auburn hair. Two old letters from John. These last things he puts carefully in a drawer. Most of the boxes are books. He stacks them against the wall, the muscles flexing in his arms. The room darkens as another cloud passes over the sun, lightens, darkens again.

Now he lies on the upholstered couch in the corner. He begins writing. He writes on a white pad of paper, wavy lines and strange signs, mathematical symbols. He closes his eyes for a while, begins writing again. Someone knocks at his door, but he doesn't hear. He imagines corrugated surfaces, magnified again and again. He calculates and imagines, while the room glows and dims and the sun slides slowly across the floor.

Dr. Lang, let me say again that it's good to have you on the faculty, says the dean. Bennett smiles. The dean, an historian, is small but long, with a thin, tubular neck that protrudes far beyond his collar. His eyes lie close together. He has the manner of an animal accustomed to darkness and damp.

A fine discipline, physics, says the dean. A fine discipline. And a fine department of physics we have here at Leominster. Bennett nods and remains standing. The dean offers the new assistant professor a licorice from a glass jar on his desk. Bennett puts it in his pocket. You like basketball? says the dean. Bennett shrugs his shoulders.

A fine department of physics we have here, the

dean repeats, playing with his pencils. Lang, you've no idea what it takes to keep a college like this afloat. The Harvards and the Yales, they can sit back on their fat, pompous reputations, and the money keeps flowing into their coffers. Arrogant sons of bitches. But a small, honest college like Leominster must continually prove its excellence. The dean pauses, eyeing Bennett carefully as if trying to decide if he understands anything besides physics. Just then, the dean spills his pencil leads on the floor. Sally, he whines loudly. A woman appears at the door. The dean looks at her, hesitates. Sally, would you run out to Sables and pick up my shirts. Certainly, Professor Kramer, says the dean's secretary. And make sure they didn't starch the shit out of them like last time, says the dean.

The dean appears to be concentrating on something. Minutes pass, or perhaps only seconds. Then he says to Bennett, Are you familiar with the work of Arnold Scalapino? Of course, Bennett answers. You know that Professor Scalapino is on our faculty, says the dean. Perhaps that's why you accepted our offer. The dean's thin lips part in a smile of satisfaction. Bennett stares at the floor. He wants only to finish unpacking his boxes and to prepare for his first classes, three days away. We have a little problem with Scalapino, continues the dean. He hasn't published anything for ten years.

## Good Benito

Bennett is well aware of Scalapino's publication record. It's part of the legend. Scalapino doesn't publish. Scholars suspect that Arnold Scalapino has performed reams of calculations, but apparently he detests to waste time writing up his results. In fact, Scalapino's entire reputation rests on two short papers from conference proceedings, one in 1959 and one in 1965. At each of those assemblies, the reclusive physicist appeared unexpectedly, delivered a terse and brilliant lecture, then vanished. Each of his two lectures, transcribed by admiring students and exhaustively studied for years, altered the course of physics in its area. A single footnote in the second paper led to what eventually became called the Scalapino quantum instability. Maddeningly, both of Scalapino's papers hinted at further, unproven results, revolutionary ideas perhaps calculated and codified on wrinkled scraps of paper lying about Scalapino's office somewhere. Or perhaps not. Scalapino himself has never been available for queries. He doesn't answer his phone.

We hired Scalapino a decade ago, says the dean softly, baring his yellow teeth. He comes to college one day a week, to preside over a seminar, and then disappears. He doesn't come to faculty meetings. He doesn't serve on committees. He doesn't supervise students. And he hasn't produced one goddamned piece of work.

That sly bastard swindled us. He talked the provost into giving him the highest salary in the college, and he hasn't published one goddamned paper. Who the hell does he think he is?

The dean slides back into his suit, then lowers his voice still further to a whisper, almost a hiss. Lang, do you understand what a Nobel Prize would mean to Leominster, what endowments we could get with a Nobel?

Is Scalapino still working? Bennett asks. Isn't he in his fifties now? The dean's eyes narrow. It doesn't matter if he's still working. What do you mean? Bennett asks. It's all in his file cabinets, says the dean. He's got twenty years of unpublished work written down and stored in his files. Bennett is stunned. Twenty years of Scalapino's work, if it truly exists, could turn modern physics on its head. The results of the first decade have probably been rediscovered by now, but those of the last could be completely unknown. Bennett cannot comprehend the possibilities. He sits down for the first time.

The dean notices his new faculty member's reaction and smiles. We know what Scalapino has been hiding from us, he says. Three years ago, I sent Garfund to Scalapino's house to talk to him. Garfund spotted the file cabinets there, in the study, crammed with pages of equations. That fool Garfund, shouts the dean. He threatened Scalapino. How could I have made such a fool the chairman of the physics department? You don't threaten a sly bastard like Scalapino. You coax him. The dean pauses. Then: Lang, I want you to go get those files. Will you do it?

Bennett has forgotten his boxes. Visions of new branches of physics flicker through his mind. Yes, he hears himself say. Yes, he will put aside his own research for several months to do this fantastic thing. Good, says the dean. You've got nine months. In May, our trustees convene, and I want to place some of Scalapino's work in their paws, ready for publication. Do you understand? You've got nine months. Bennett nods.

Good, repeats the dean. I correctly sized you up as an intelligent young man. Scalapino lives in Fells Point. Here's his address. The dean scribbles something on a piece of paper and hands it to the young physicist.

A week later, Bennett makes his first visit to Scalapino's house in east Baltimore, near the harbor. He parks his car and walks up the street. Red-brick row houses nestle oddly between bars, shoe shops, cafés, glass companies, bookstores, pizza parlors. Artists and musicians live in Fells Point, in a great cauldron of ethnic groups: Germans, Italians, Poles, American Indians. Being near the ocean, the area provides a natural entry point for immigrants. And the seamen come ashore. The streets are littered with bars like the Horse You Came in On and the Cat's Eye Pub. Shouts and saxophone music pour out from open windows and the air is warm and Bennett's shoes click pleasantly as he walks. The streets are paved in Belgian block, a smooth kind of cobblestone once used for ballast in the great sailing ships.

He stops at a three-story red brick house on Aliceanna Street. A rusting metal gate stands in front of half the house, leaving the other half exposed to the street. It is midafternoon. He knocks for a long time. He knocks and sweats a little in the warm air and only half-believes he is standing at Arnold Scalapino's house when a pretty, dark-haired woman in her late twenties finally answers the door, opens it just enough to see him. I'm Bennett Lang, the new assistant professor at Leominster, he says smiling. I've come to see Professor Scalapino. What do you want with him? says the young woman, he's very busy. I just wanted to say hello, Bennett says anxiously. He's busy, the young woman repeats and closes the door firmly.

Bennett goes back to his cramped office at Leominster. He pulls down the blinds and lies on his couch. He begins examining the cracks in the ceiling. They branch out like tributaries of a river, or veins of a leaf. They wander, connect, then separate again, delicate patterns unobserved until this moment. Who is that woman who guards Scalapino? Through the crack in the doorframe, he saw she was holding a book. Perhaps she is a reader. He will buy her a copy of Lucien's *Tactile Mountains* and return to Fells Point.

Mr. Lang again, the young woman says, irritated. I told you he's busy. Good afternoon, Mr. Lang. She begins closing the door. At least she remembered his name. Bennett quickly thrusts the book through the crack in the door, into her hand. She looks at it. Her frown softens. May I come back? he blurts out. She hesitates, looks again at the book, then at Bennett. A man's voice, baritone and distant, floats from a neighboring house. Try next Thursday, after ten in the evening, she says and shuts the door. Bennett strides happily around the half-gate and spends an hour walking through the cobblestone streets. On some impulse, he buys a green crystal thimble.

Fells Point at night is alive. Men and women drift singly and in pairs through the streets. Music floats in the warm, colored air. Two women with shopping bags argue loudly under a streetlamp. A man staggers under the weight of three cases of Shawney Girl beer.

The woman in Scalapino's house lets Bennett in. She introduces herself as Sophie, Scalapino's daughter, and leads Bennett up a curving flight of stairs. It is narrow and close and the walls are decorated with pages from an old calculus book. After reaching the top, Sophie turns left, and they immediately enter a kitchen smelling of smoked herring. There, bent over the kitchen table with a pad of white paper, is a monstrously fat man. Arnold Scalapino. He seems wedged in his seat, his huge belly straining upward against the underside of the table. Great rolls of pink flesh hang around his neck. He looks up when Bennett walks in and indicates with his huge hand that he should move to the other end of the table.

Bennett sits down and fiercely pinches his leg under the table. Yes, I'd heard there was a new man in the department, says Scalapino. Now we're back up to three. His voice is surprisingly high-pitched. Sophie leans against an old Westinghouse refrigerator, watching them. Uh, I just finished my doctoral work at Blaine, with Davis Jacoby, says Bennett, praying that Scalapino will recognize the name of his thesis advisor. Ah, yes, Davis Jacoby, Scalapino squeaks. He did some fine work on space-time singularities. Tell me about your thesis problem. Scalapino waves the young physicist to the blackboard that stands oddly in the corner of the kitchen.

Bennett has lectured on his thesis many times before. He picks up the chalk and his fright disappears. But he has barely begun when Scalapino asks him two questions. The first question he answers without trouble. The second he struggles with. Scalapino has swiftly bracketed Bennett's knowledge. After the second question and Bennett's labored reply, the older man snorts, drops his huge head, and resumes pondering the equations on his white pad of paper. He does not look up again. After a minute, Sophie politely informs Bennett that her father is now occupied and she will show him to the door. The interview has lasted fifteen minutes.

He withdraws. He disappears into the sleepy folds of the college, happy to be alone in this town where he knows no one, to return to his own work and his solitude. He again takes up his calculations. He counts cracks on the ceiling in his office. He goes to his classes, meets with his students on the small upholstered couch. The air turns cooler and he begins wearing his green jacket and noticing the blood-red leaves of the maple outside his window. Several times over the next couple of months, he goes back to 137 Aliceanna Street on Thursday evenings. Each time, he is turned away at the door by Scalapino's daughter, who repeats that her father is busy or thinking or otherwise occupied.

In late November, Sophie unexpectedly lets Bennett in, as if no time has passed. She takes him up the winding stairway with the equations on the wall. The kitchen is empty. He stands alone at the top of the landing, Sophie having vanished, when he hears a squeal. It is Scalapino, saying, Now that is a nontrivial move. Following the voice, Bennett walks down a long hallway and into a brightly lit room, where he discovers ten chess games in progress. Scalapino is studying one of the boards, grinning broadly. A nontrivial move, he repeats. Against one wall sits a computer. Scalapino is playing the computer. Sophie, who soon comes to the door, explains that her father has programmed the computer to generate moves from random numbers, subject only to the rules of the game and the current positions of the pieces. The vast majority of random moves are preposterously silly, but every once in a while the computer makes a truly brilliant choice, which keeps Scalapino engaged for half an hour. Evidently, such a profound accident has just occurred.

After a few minutes, Scalapino looks up from his board. You're persistent, Lang. But not offensive. I like that. Bennett decides to seize his opportunity. He states his mission, tactfully but with no wasted words. Scalapino looks at him suspiciously.

Bennett's eyes wander. From where he is standing, he can see across the hall into another room, dimly lit, and thinks he can make out the shadowy shape of a file cabinet.

My notes are only for my own pleasure, says Scalapino. Then you do have notes? Bennett says, unable to blunt his excitement. Yes, says Scalapino, waving carelessly in the direction of the other room, But I'm not interested in dollying up my notes. Once I see how to get to the end of a problem, it's time to start something new. That's the fun of it.

Scalapino immediately begins telling Bennett about his current project, something called string theory, dealing with subatomic physics. Bennett cannot think about string theory at this moment. He pleads again with the great physicist. You don't realize the importance of your work, he says. I'll go through your notes, I'll write the papers for you. It would be an honor.

Scalapino snorts and rotates the great dome on his shoulders and exchanges glances with his daughter. A tentative look comes over his pasty white face. So you were a student of Jacoby's? he says. Bennett nods. Scalapino looks again at his daughter. He scratches his eyebrows. All right, he sighs. All right. But the files don't leave the house. Sophie, take Dr. Lang to the study and show him the files. Then Scalapino stands up and waddles down the hall to the kitchen and his white pad of paper.

Bennett follows Sophie into the study. There they are. Scalapino's files. He opens the first file. It is labeled Radiation from Accelerated Event Horizons and contains many pages of equations. He opens the second: Percolation in N Dimensions. More pages of calculations. A third: Modifications in the Wheeler-DeWitt Equation for Quantum Superspace. Bennett sinks into a chair, unable to speak. You look tired, says Sophie. Come back tomorrow night.

The next night, Sophie takes Bennett immediately to Scalapino's study. In the lamplight, he can see that back issues of the *Physical Review* are piled up on the windowsill, on the desk, on the floor. Shoes are used as bookends, often not in matching pairs. Unopened letters from Lapides, Mortenheim, Kaiser, Temin litter the desk. Jars of peanut butter sit in half-open drawers.

Bennett pulls out the first file and starts to read. The pages are wrinkled and darkened with coffee stains and not in any order. Mathematics dominates the words, which peer tentatively between equations like timid forest animals. Most of these few furtive words are of the species of It obviously follows that, or Thus, or An excellent approximation is. Bennett stares out the window, at the streetlights below, and realizes that he will have to rederive the equations. It will be tedious and difficult, for Scalapino has skipped many steps between one equation and the next. And there are none of the usual references to prior results or articles in journals.

Indeed, as Bennett soon learns, Scalapino hardly ever reads the scientific literature. When he does, he looks at a paper only long enough to see what the problem is, then quickly shuts the journal, as if having glanced at an unwanted review of a film, and derives all the results on his own. On the rare occasions that he travels, he is besieged in hallways and even restrooms by other physicists, who are anxious to discuss their latest discoveries with him. After a very few minutes, they often find to their horror that Scalapino not only understands their new results, but has already calculated far more general results, which he keeps in his file drawer and hasn't bothered to publish. This annoys some of his colleagues. Taped to the wall of Scalapino's study is a five-year-old letter from Lapides that reads simply, Fuck You.

Bennett has been engrossed in the files for a couple of hours when the house begins shaking and rumbling. He leaps from the chair, thinking an earthquake has hit. Sophie arrives and says that a freight train is passing, a regular evening event. The trains, which carry chemicals, move very slowly and leave a fine yellow powder on the windowsills in the morning. She looks down at the desk and Bennett's work. I'm glad you're doing this, she says softly, and then leaves. Bennett is exhausted. Apparently Scalapino and his daughter sleep during the day and stay up all night, but he is not used to these hours. He goes home to his small apartment near campus, elated but worried.

The next day, at the college, he finds a note in his mail slot, from the dean. It says, Do you have the files? May is fast approaching. Please drop by my office at your earliest convenience. Bennett has no intention of dropping by the dean's office. In his classes that day, he feels inspired. He has gotten a glimpse of the work of a great physicist. With unusual enthusiasm, he describes to his pupils the beauty of Newton's three laws of motion. His students look at him uncomprehendingly, like cows at a passing train.

It snows. Snow is unusual for Baltimore. The streets remain buried under white blankets, the few cars that venture forth collide with each other or slide off the road. The city turns silent and white. At midday, Bennett manages to find one undaunted bus that is traveling to Fells Point. He goes to 137 Aliceanna, arriving in broad daylight for the first time in months.

He hears shouts. To his surprise, he sees Scalapino and Sophie awake and out in the street, throwing snowballs at each other and screeching like children. Scalapino wears a red woolen cap with a tassel on top. Bennett joins them. Despite his obvious pleasure, Scalapino moves slowly and with great labor, his various sweaters and scarfs bulging like drawers from a huge chest being dragged across a room. After a few minutes, he is sweating heavily and panting, and his face is as red as his hat. He sits down. You're a pretty good shot, Lang, he says after his hard breathing subsides. And I'm a pretty good target. He releases a high-noted giggle and pats Bennett on the back. Bennett doesn't work on the equations that evening. Instead, he and Sophie discuss Lucien and Calvino while Scalapino plays chess with his computer.

Then, Christmas vacation. Scalapino and Sophie disappear on some undisclosed trip. It is January before Bennett sees them again. When they return, he begins following the hours of the house, sleeping by day, whenever he isn't teaching, and working through the night in Scalapino's study. He finally gives up on the first file and moves to the second. Again, the pages are jumbled. He cannot follow all the mathematics. There are occasional strange diagrams that make no sense to him. Some of the calculations are written on scraps of grocery lists and electric bills and restaurant place mats. He has battled for six weeks with Scalapino's notes, and he has amassed the heaviest armaments he can find: volume two of Bjorken and Drell's *Relativistic Quantum Mechanics,* Gill and Thurbach's *Advanced Methods of Mathematical Physics,* Hammermold's *Differential Geometry and Tensor Analysis.*

One day, around three in the morning, he can bear it no longer. He goes to the kitchen and asks Scalapino for help. The huge physicist sits at the table with his eyes closed like a meditating Buddha, pure in his habitual white shirt. His closet is full of white shirts, simplifying the problem of matching ensembles. The younger man coughs, places the pile of raggedy pages down on the table, and points imploringly at a flock of equations that have seemingly migrated from nowhere. Scalapino glances at them out of the corner of his eye. Percolation, he squeaks, that was 1969. He waves the pages away. Sophie, who has been reading a novel in the next room, overhears the conversation and calls to her father. Daddy, try to help. Father and daughter argue. Finally Scalapino yells, Strings, strings, I'm working on strings. I've done percolation. I'm bored with percolation.

Bennett silently gathers up the indecipherable runes of what is probably the definitive theory of percolation and retreats to the study. The streetlights shine sharply in the cold air outside. He clears a space on the desk and puts his head down and releases the grip on his pencil. Later, he discusses the matter with Sophie. She spends a long time with her father in the kitchen. Finally she returns to the study, where Bennett still slumps at the desk. I'm terribly sorry, Bennett, she says sadly. I'm sorry for everyone. My father apologizes to you, but he simply can't force himself to go back to what he's already accomplished. He's been this way for many years. I can't explain it to you. He sincerely apologizes, but he can't do it. But he hopes you will keep coming to the house. He likes you. Bennett raises his head and nods. He is beginning to realize that

Scalapino's twenty years of notes will remain forever imprisoned within the walls of this room. And he will go back to his own career, publishing lesser works in profusion.


He lies on the sofa in his small office, staring at the cracks on the ceiling, searching for patterns. He has never given up on a problem, he has always found some solution. He searches for patterns and decides that he should propose a new project to Scalapino, a collaboration, a physics problem that Bennett understands from the start. Nothing so grand as string theory, but something substantial. Perhaps the older physicist could spend a few minutes with him here and there. In the past, even when Scalapino worked on seemingly mundane problems, he often uncovered luminescent depths.

The great physicist will have to get interested. Bennett starts with his thesis work on gravitational radiation. This time, however, it is he who asks the questions. They sit in the brightly lit chess room with the computer and the random numbers. Scalapino looks up from his chessboard, frowns, and returns to the game. It's an intriguing question, don't you think, says Bennett, the amount of free energy in a radiating system?

Intriguing perhaps, but shallow, says Scalapino as he walks over to feed the computer his latest move. It could, perhaps, involve the cosmic entropy problem, says Bennett. Bennett is desperately grasping at straws, but he knows that a mere mention of the entropy in the universe causes physicists to skip meals and remain glued to the blackboard for hours. No one has ever solved the problem of why the universe was created in such a high state of order. Scalapino frowns again. He stops looking at the chessboards. He seems distracted and his eyes slowly turn glassy. Then he goes to the kitchen, Bennett following behind. He paces. Without saying a word, he begins drawing pictures and bits of equations on the blackboard. He is caught.

After considerable effort, Bennett gets an explanation. Immediately, he copies everything down and hurries off to the study to add his own contribution, which consists of carefully verifying the first equation, describing in words the physical picture behind it, and copying everything over in a neat and well-documented form. After an hour or so, he returns to the kitchen, where Scalapino is scribbling furiously on his white pad of paper. What the hell is this? Scalapino says, reading what Bennett has written. Take it out. Why? Bennett asks. Because it's imprecise, Scalapino squeaks. You get into trouble when you use words. Words are ambiguous. Mathematics is not. But, Bennett protests, you yourself described a physical picture, with waves. Scalapino shakes his great head. The waves helped me get started, he says. But now we've got the differential equation. The mathematics is precise. Stick with the mathematics.

At which point Scalapino effortlessly writes down more equations, which flow from his pencil like water from a spring. What are you thinking? Bennett asks in amazement. Thinking? says Scalapino. I'm thinking that the cubic term will dominate in the near-field zone and the quadratic in the far-field. We might have to shoot to match boundary conditions.

Scalapino floats in some netherworld, half of the body and half of the mind. He can no more describe to Bennett what he is thinking than a great ballerina can say how she does a pirouette. Bennett takes Scalapino's new scribblings off to the study to purify. In an hour he returns. They repeat the process. From time to time, the house rumbles with a passing train, Sophie brings tea, Scalapino lumbers down the hall to the chess room.

The collaboration goes on in this manner for a couple of months. Bennett comes to the house several times a week. Sometimes he brings new novels for Sophie, sometimes moo shu chicken and pea pods from the Happy Palace in Fells Point. Sometimes he sleeps on a cot in the study. Occasionally he is able to go the next mathematical step without help from Scalapino, and the great physicist nods and smiles at his assistant's new result. The pages accumulate. And Bennett has managed to negotiate a small amount of text to accompany the equations, for the slow readers of the *Physical Review*.

It is near dawn. The three of them sprawl languidly in separate chairs, shadows in the low light of a single porcelain lamp. They sit in Sophie's reading room, full of her books. Scalapino comes here with his daughter some mornings before bed. No one has spoken for minutes. It is dead quiet. Far away, a voice floats through the walls of the house, Ella Fitzgerald singing Do Nothing till You Hear from Me. The voice swims through the silent air, and Bennett thinks of Memphis and of Florida singing her slow, heavyhearted songs at the ironing board. Who's playing the record? he asks. Sophie shrugs her shoulders. We don't know our neighbors, she says.

They sit half asleep, listening to the voice in the distance. Finally, Sophie stands up and stretches. I'm going to bed, she says, yawning. She kisses her father and goes to her bedroom.

I wish she would find a life of her own, Scalapino

says quietly, after she's gone. I've talked to her. I wish she would do something. But she won't leave me. He smiles sadly, then leans back in a pillow. In minutes, he is asleep. Bennett walks over and places the green quilt around his huge body, then walks soundlessly down the stairs.

In the middle of April, just before dawn, they finish. To solve the last equation, they've been obliged to enlist Scalapino's computer. The final result is a single number five digits long. Scalapino would have liked more digits, but his computer didn't have the accuracy.

Bennett drives slowly back to campus, watching the tops of trees start to glow in the east and the paperboys making their deliveries and the dogs stretching and waiting at the doors for their breakfasts. He is too agitated and excited to go to his apartment to sleep. So he goes to his office on campus, to the upholstered couch. Lying there, he contemplates the number, repeating it over and over. It is a beautiful number. He closes his eyes and is surprised to see the faces of Scalapino and Sophie and the kitchen with the blackboard in the corner and Scalapino waddling down the hall and Sophie's room in the dim light of dawn and the music, and it seems that all of his life for the last half a year has been squeezed and distilled into one lovely number. He smiles and he drifts off to sleep.

A week later, the research paper has been typed and is ready to send to the journal. Bennett sits in the octagonal reference room of the science library, checking a final notation. Looking up at a nearby shelf, he happens to glance at a recent issue of *Nuova Physica,* an obscure Italian physics journal. In its table of contents is a title similar to that for his paper with Scalapino.

His pulse races. He roughly takes the magazine off the stand, flies through the article, turning pages rapidly, and jumps to the end. The final number is the same as his to five digits.

In a state of confusion, he drives to Scalapino's house. It is the middle of the afternoon. Sophie comes to the door sleepily. She recognizes his urgency and agrees to wake her father. Scalapino plods to the kitchen in his pajamas, not yet awake. Look at this, Bennett shouts, handing him the volume of *Nuova Physica.* Scalapino stares at the paper for a few minutes, nods, and says, His method is clumsy. Least action is more elegant. Look at his answer, Bennett explodes. It's identical to ours to five digits. Scalapino shrugs his shoulders. So what? he says. What did you expect? The Italian solved the same problem. It's a well-posed problem. He should get the same answer. I'm going back to bed. Scalapino yawns and moves for the hallway. Exactly the same to five digits, Bennett repeats miserably. It would have been seven if the 360 had more memory, says Scalapino. Or twelve. It's a perfectly well-posed problem. Now please excuse me, I'm going to bed.

Bennett stumbles from the house. He wanders through the side streets of Fells Point for the rest of the day, finally remembers his car, and returns to his apartment, profoundly empty. Years later, he will not remember whether he ever said goodbye to Sophie.

May came and went. Bennett never heard from the dean. The dean had received an offer from Harvard and left with the first bloom of the lilacs.

**B**ennett's earliest memory is a sound, the sound of Florida singing. Florida was the black maid who worked for his family in Memphis and raised him and his brothers from birth. In the farthest reaches of his mind, Bennett remembers lying somewhere in the house and hearing that voice floating from the kitchen, where Florida was usually ironing shirts at her ironing board. Oh, sweet Jesus, my Savior, I'm coming home to you. He might have been two years old. Florida would have been in her early thirties at the time. She belonged to a Baptist church on Chelsea and sang in the church choir. Bennett didn't understand the words, but he felt the comfort. Florida's song, like the air, was always there, filling the rooms of the house. It was slow and lilting and sad, and it had strength. Her voice rolled over Bennett in waves. Her voice lulled him to sleep and gently woke him from his naps. Her voice was so constant and soothing that he felt something was wrong when he didn't hear it. Oh, sweet Jesus, I'm coming home to you.

Florida worked long hours. She came around 7:00 in the morning and left around 7:30 in the evening, often six days a week. She always wore a white uniform in the house. When she arrived in the morning, coming in through the back of the house, she would stop in the utility room off the kitchen and change from her own clothes into the uniform hanging in the closet. Then, before leaving at night, she would change back into her own clothes.

Florida did all the housework. She cooked. She ironed. She cleaned and she vacuumed. Bennett's mother always suspected that Florida neglected the upstairs because she didn't like mounting the steps. Florida was enormously fat, even when she was younger, and she had a hard time walking. Bennett made his own bed, and when he saw dust and dirt up there he kept quiet about it.

In the first years, in addition to cleaning, Florida helped get the boys dressed in the morning, made them their breakfast, and drove them to school. Bennett and his brothers attended a suburban public school a couple of miles from their house. Florida would let the boys off across the street, next to a laundromat with a blue sign that said Same Day Service and a Rexall drugstore. As they got older, the brothers walked to school, but when they were young, Florida drove them. Maids who could drive, like Florida, were especially prized.

Bennett remembers many times coming home from school and burying his head in Florida's huge bosom after he'd scraped his leg or another boy had said something mean. She would say, Tell me 'bout it, honey, tell Florida. And he would feel better. He was certain that Florida loved him and his brothers. Their mother loved them too, but Florida gave them a clear, unquestioning love. She never took sides, especially in family arguments, but she made the children feel better. On those evenings when Bennett's parents went out, Florida told stories. It would be before bedtime, after the children had gotten into their pajamas, and Bennett and his brothers would curl up around her on the beige couch in the family room. Most of the stories were from the Bible. Florida didn't put much religion into the stories, but there was always a moral.

The most important thing in Florida's life, outside the Lang family, was her church. It was surprising to Bennett that she had any other life at all. She worked such long hours, and she was employed by Bennett's family thirty-five years. For a brief time, she was married to a man named Quentin. She said little about Quentin. I ain't met no good men, and I ain't wasting my time on them no-'count men anymore, she often said, sitting at the table and drinking an RC Cola. If anyone called Florida during the day, other than the credit union, it was a friend to talk about church business. Bennett never knew much about what Florida did at her church, but he knew that she was devoted to it. On Thursday or Friday of each week, she would start moving around the house with a little extra speed.

One day when his parents were out of town on a long trip and his Aunt Mamie was staying at the house, Bennett got a terrible fever. He was so weak that he couldn't get out of bed to go to the toilet. He just lay on his back, staring at the brass chandelier on the ceiling. He was sick for a week. Every afternoon of that week, Florida gave him an alcohol bath and put wet towels on his forehead. Wet towels were her favorite remedy for fevers. For stomachaches, she gave hot tea with sassafras. Florida had a powerful dislike of doctors. They always poking you and sticking you and talking like they know something, she would say. She used the same remedies for her own frequent ailments. Until the end of her life, she never set foot in a doctor's office, much less a hospital.

The Sunday that Bennett was so ill, Florida had a big church function, which she'd been talking about for months. It was a barbecue and songfest with some out-of-town gospel singers. Florida had never traveled beyond Memphis, and she could hardly imagine a joint choir made out of her own church group and these top-drawer gospel singers from Nashville. She hummed and sang and bought a new pair of earrings for the occasion. Saturday came around, the day before the big event, and Bennett was still sick. Then, early Sunday morning, he heard Florida's heavy footsteps trudging up the stairs. A knock on his door. She was dressed in her Sunday clothes. But she wasn't going to the songfest. She sat at Bennett's bedside all day, putting wet towels on his forehead. He'd never seen Florida in the house not wearing her white uniform. In the afternoon, Aunt Mamie bustled into Bennett's room, squinted at Florida, and said, Shouldn't you change clothes, Florida? Today is my day off, Miz Edelson, answered Florida.


It was Florida who usually revived Bennett's mother when she fainted. This would happen about once a month, generally in the midst of a big row between the three boys. Bennett's mother had wanted a daughter so badly. And the boys were always fighting. She tried to keep peace, but she would often just throw up her hands and start shouting. She didn't like to shout. Southern ladies didn't shout. But she would be driven to it, and she would finally throw up her hands and shout, I'm going to tell your father about this when he gets home. An invocation of Bennett's father was, in fact, a weak threat. When Bennett's father got home from work, he would always cloister himself in the living room with a book for the evening, joining the family for dinner and then returning to his book. With the instrument of punishment thus diminished, Mrs. Lang's threats rolled off the backs of her children. They would keep fighting, and she would yell and get upset at herself for yelling and work herself into an awful state of agitation and start hyperventilating and faint. Mother's fainted, the children would bawl, and Florida would go to the medicine cabinet and get out the smelling salts. When Bennett's mother came to, still on the floor, she would say, Where am I? You fainted again, Miz Lang, answered Florida, hovering over her with the smelling salts and gently holding her hand. The boys would feel terribly guilty when their mother fainted and try to temper themselves for the rest of the day. As they got older, they sometimes thought that their mother fainted intentionally, for dramatic effect.

Bennett's mother had a secret life at night. She was an insomniac. During the wee hours, she roamed through the house, looking through drawers, writing notes to herself, reading unusual books. Her wanderings always ended up in the kitchen, where her willpower would succumb to her exhaustion and she would eat anything in sight, especially leftover desserts. She could easily consume two thirds of a pie, or two pints of ice cream, or eight chocolate brownies. Over the years, her lack of control in the night led to a running cat-and-mouse game with Florida.

Each evening after dinner, she would ask Florida to hide the desserts. Florida stashed desserts in the washing machine, in drawers, in closets, under the couch. She would look at Bennett with an embarrassed grin and say, That's what Miz Lang tell me to do. Now don't you tell Miz Lang where I'm puttin' this apple pie. Next morning, the apple pie would be gone. Bennett's mother would come into the kitchen and scold Florida for not hiding the pie well enough. Florida would grimace with hurt and that night would hide the dessert exceedingly well. The next morning, Bennett's mother would come into the kitchen and not say anything to

Florida, not even good morning. That night, Florida would again hide the dessert with extra care. Next morning, Bennett's mother would come into the kitchen even more silent and grumpy. Florida would glance at her sheepishly, but Mrs. Lang wouldn't look at Florida at all. After a few days of this treatment, Florida would crumble. But Miz Lang, she would blurt out, you asked me to hide the dessert so you couldn't find it. Bennett's mother would gaze out the window at some faraway object and whisper, in the slow, southern way of talking, But I didn't ask you to hide it like that. At these words, Florida would get a puzzled look on her face, her eyes would get very big, and that night she would hide the dessert where any amateur could find it. The next morning, Bennett's mother would seem satisfied. But after a few mornings of that satisfied look, she would get angry all over again, again chew out Florida for not hiding the desserts, and the entire cycle would repeat. From the mood of the house, Bennett could always tell whether it was a day when Florida was hiding the desserts too well or not well enough.

Most of the desserts in question were made by Florida herself. Florida was a wonderful cook. She was so good that Bennett's mother sometimes lent her out to her friends for dinner parties. Bennett was in the kitchen on more than one occasion when his mother entreated Florida not to reveal the ingredients of her barbecue sauce to anyone, especially not to her friends' maids.

What Bennett and his brothers loved best, what they thought about all day when they knew it was imminent, was Florida's karo pecan pie. Her pecan pie had big chunks of pecans, often taken right from their own pecan tree. The filling was soft and gooey and sweet, but not too sweet. She made her own piecrust from flour and lard and rolled the crusts very thin on the kitchen counter. Bennett's mother closed her eyes while she was eating Florida's karo pecan pie. Bennett and his brothers kept their eyes open and ate as fast as they could, so that they might get seconds. They usually asked for a scoop of vanilla ice cream on top. What y'all need ice cream for on that good pie? Florida would say. Then she would sigh and look at them mournfully and put the ice cream on as requested.

While the family ate together in the dining room, Florida sat in the adjoining kitchen. When something was needed, Bennett's mother shook a little brass bell. Florida would come into the dining room through the swinging door saying, Yes'um, Miz Lang, and bring more water or an extra fork or more lamb chops. Where are the turnip greens? Bennett's mother might ask Florida when she came in. I didn't know you

wanted turnip greens, Miz Lang, Florida would answer,
I made lima beans. I wanted lima beans *and* turnip
greens, Bennett's mother would say. I wrote turnip
greens down on the menu. Didn't you read the menu?
I'm sorry, Miz Lang, Florida would say and then turn
around and go back through the swinging door. Between rings of the bell, she ate her own dinner alone at
the kitchen table.

After dinner, the family would go about their
evening activities while Florida cleaned up the dishes.
When Bennett got older and occasionally went to a
school dance, he always arranged to bring his date by
the house early in the evening, while Florida was still
there. Florida would pretend she was engaged with the
dishes, but she would get a real good look at Bennett's
new girl and prick up her ears at any words from the
young lady's mouth. Minutes later, as Bennett was leaving through the back door of the kitchen, Florida would
sneak him a quick glance from over by the sink. Sometimes she grinned approvingly and nodded her head
yes. Sometimes she frowned and shook her head no.
She never said anything to the young women, except
once, when she mentioned to Susan Caldwell that Bennett was going to be another Thomas Edison.

• • •

Florida's last name was Wicker. Florida Wicker. The only time Bennett heard her last name spoken was when people from the credit union called up and asked to speak to Florida Wicker. Her debt quietly tormented her, and she constantly dreaded that the few items she owned would be reclaimed. She didn't get paid much by the Langs. They paid her about thirty-five dollars per week in the early 1960s, before the minimum-wage laws. That was the going rate for black help at the time.

Florida spent a large part of her income on cigarettes. She smoked Pall Malls. She was a chain-smoker, except when she was singing, and she got great comfort from her cigarettes. In her forties, she began to suffer various respiratory problems. She knew that smoking was bad for her health and that she couldn't afford it, but it was one of her few pleasures and she never gave it up. She spent the last two months of her life lying on her back in a hospital, too weak to protest, unable to sit up, a tube in her trachea, a dialysis machine pumping her kidneys, balloons around her legs to keep them from swelling. When he heard she was dying, Bennett wept inside of himself, but he didn't go to the hospital. He couldn't bear to see Florida like that.

The last time he saw her was several years earlier, the only time he visited her in her own house, on Harrison Street in north Memphis. He had been living in Baltimore and hadn't seen Florida for some time. She still worked for his parents, although now only one day a week. It was a sweltering day in July. He discovered that she lived in a tiny brick house, wedged in a row of other tiny brick houses. The houses all had two steps up to the door and screen porches with clotheslines strung across them. Florida's car, a beat-up blue Plymouth that Bennett's parents had given her after owning it themselves, was parked out in front. Down the street, an awning cranked. Smells of barbecued chicken wafted through the air.

When Bennett opened the screen door to her porch, Florida was sitting in a white aluminum lawn chair. The top of her dress was soaked with perspiration and clung to her skin. She broke out in a grin when she saw him. Ain't this heat something awful, she said, mopping up her forehead with a handkerchief. Bennett nodded and smiled. Lord, let me look at you, she said. Her emphysema was bad, and she wheezed when she spoke. You sure is grown-up now, she said. Way grown-up. Are you happy, baby? Bennett was startled by her question and found that he couldn't answer it.

Through the years, he had often tried to imagine Florida's house. He wondered what her own kitchen looked like. He wondered whether she had pictures of Jesus on the walls, whether she had photographs of him and his brothers, whether she had a television, or a big shaggy rug. He wondered what her house smelled like. But she never took him inside. They sat on her porch for an hour and talked about him and his brothers and her church, and he left.

W hen Bennett was ten or eleven he converted a large storage closet off his room into a laboratory and stocked it with batteries, wires, capacitors, test tubes, Bunsen burners, bottles of sulfuric acid—all neatly organized in labeled plastic boxes on white vinyl shelves. Bennett's younger brothers, Marty and Philip, were always prowling around his laboratory. He had to keep it locked with a big silver Yale lock. The key to the lock he kept hidden inside his stuffed frog from Acapulco, given to him by his Uncle Malcolm. His brothers detested that stuffed frog and wouldn't go near it.

Most of Bennett's scientific projects began with a sudden mental image of a gadget that could do something interesting. Then he would decide he had to build that gadget. He never had any grand notions of uncovering the secrets of the universe. He would simply get this sudden vision in his head and feel a powerful urge to create it.

He dedicated an entire Christmas vacation to building a remote-control system that would allow him to turn on the lights of his room from anywhere in the house. To fool around with the wires to the light switch he had to shut off the main power to the house, an operation most wisely accomplished when his parents weren't home. Child, you sure getting into some high cotton now, Florida said. You're going into some trouble this time. But after a while, Florida calmed down and helpfully took Bennett's brothers out for a walk. When they returned, Bennett was already howling with excitement as he raced around the house trying out his invention from every possible location. It's on! shouted one of his brothers from upstairs in Bennett's room. It's off! On! You sure is something, child, Florida said smiling, you're going to be Thomas Edison.

At times, Bennett's creativity was sparked by small domestic troubles. Once, after years of making himself hoarse yelling downstairs to summon his brothers up to his room, he unexpectedly visualized a system of speakers and wires emanating outward from his room and traveling downstairs to theirs. He built it, and it worked pretty well, though not perfectly. The amplifier injected a background hum into the system, so that he had to shout into the microphone to be heard at the other end of the line. His brothers, however, were mightily impressed.

Bennett was fascinated by some of the images in the movie *Frankenstein,* especially the lightning-like discharges leaping between electrodes. This was a phenomenon worth looking into. After some research, he learned that Dr. Frankenstein's electrical machine was called an induction coil. He built one. It involved wrapping wire around an electromagnet. A pulsating electric current traveling through the core of the magnet caused its magnetism to ebb and flow, like the tides, in turn generating an enormous voltage in the circumscribing coils of wire. According to the laws of physics, which Bennett had read in a book, the more turns of wire around the magnet, the greater the voltage. He wanted as much voltage as possible, so he decided to wrap wire until his arm dropped off. He wrapped wire for two weeks. He wrapped two miles of wire around that magnet. It was number thirty gauge, the thinnest wire available in the electrical supply stores in Memphis.

Halfway through, the wrapping got so tedious that he had to call John Lerner for help. John was

Bennett's best friend and a year older. He came over on his bike. Nice coils, Good Benito, John said approvingly. John never called Bennett by his real name. He always called him Good Benito. Nice coils, Good Benito. John studied the situation, went into Bennett's attic, and emerged with a fishing rod and reel. These he reengineered and hooked to the apparatus so that Bennett could lie on his bed and watch television while effortlessly wrapping wire with great speed.

By the time he was up to several thousand volts, he decided to quit. The electric spark in his induction coil could jump nearly an inch through the air—admittedly not as far as Dr. Frankenstein's, but he had built it himself, and he showed it off to anyone who came to the house.

When *Sputnik* orbited the earth, Bennett became agitated and transfixed with the idea of sending a projectile aloft, into the clouds and beyond. He imagined countless launches, graceful trajectories through space, silver steel reflecting the sun. However, for several years he was forced to postpone his plans to build his own rocket. The owner of Clark and Wilson's refused to sell Bennett the chemicals he needed for his rocket fuel. Finally, one summer, Mr. Clark capitulated, persuaded by Bennett's deepening voice and look of extreme seriousness.

For the next few weeks, Bennett experimented with fuels, varying a recipe of charcoal, potassium nitrate, and sulfur he'd found in *Popular Science*. A mixture that burned too fast would explode like a bomb, too slow and it would smolder like a barbecue grill. Alternating bangs and fizzles issued forth from Bennett's laboratory as he worked with tiny amounts of the mixtures.

To ignite the fuel, Bennett devised an electrical system. This was a breakthrough. He'd had bad experiences with holding a match up to gunpowder in ant holes. For this rocket job, Bennett used a flashbulb. Its sudden heat, embedded inside the fuel, was enough to start the combustion, and he could set off the bulb from great distance with long wires and a battery. These experiments, like the remote-control lighting system, were carried out when his parents were away, and he bribed his brothers to stay quiet with a shiny capacitor for each of them. For their own protection, Marty and Philip had to remain on the other side of the door while he carried out his investigations. Florida stood at the bottom of the stairs, wringing her hands and calling up, You sure getting into some high cotton now.

Eventually satisfied that he had a fuel with good thrust and a trustworthy ignition system, Bennett set about constructing the body of the craft. This he made out of a strong aluminum tube from a hardware store. He allowed Marty and Philip to put one decal each on the fuselage. Marty, the older of his brothers, proposed that the rocket have a live passenger, a lizard. Bennett designed a capsule inside the fuselage to house the animal. The lizard was to be ejected at the apogee of the orbit, triggered by a mercury switch, and to float down to earth in a parachuted container. As it turned out, Marty's specifications for the lizard weren't precisely right. Its tail stuck through the bottom of the capsule, down into the fuel chamber, and was burned off in the launch.

Finally came the fins and nose cone. These were easy. The rocket was silver, its tail fins were red. It was beautiful.

News of the project spread through the neighborhood. By the day of the launch, which took place one Saturday at dawn in the middle of the fifth hole of the Galloway Golf Course, Bennett had an audience of maybe ten kids in addition to his two brothers. John, of course, was there. John brought a folding chair and binoculars. Before launch, he walked up to Bennett and solemnly shook his hand, then installed himself in his chair and practiced rapid scans with his binoculars, jerking his gaze from the launching pad to somewhere past Alpha Centauri.

Bennett had built the launching pad out of a V-shaped steel girder, pointed skyward at the appropriate angle and anchored in a wood Coca-Cola case filled with concrete. The rocket sat nose up on the girder, the ignition wires trailing from its tail to the command center, several hundred feet away. There, in the command center, next to the firing button, Bennett stood alone. It was an early morning in September and the grass glistened with dew and the sun was coming up orange over the treetops. In the silence just before launch, Bennett could hear the faint drone of a golf cart at hole number one.

The blastoff was flawless. However, after streaking upward a mere two hundred feet, the rocket veered wildly to the east, did a sickening loop, and crashed. Bennett shrieked and slapped his hands over his eyes. The cause of the disaster was immediately obvious, even to his brothers. The rocket's tail fins had come off within a microsecond after launch, as if they'd been simply stuck on with Elmer's glue. Which they had. With appalling clarity, Bennett remembered that he had not fastened the tail fins with metal bolts but had glued them on quickly so that he could admire the finished craft. His rocket worked on the ground, but not in the air.

**J**ohn Lerner was an only child, physically fragile, and, like Bennett, a boy of few words. John did, however, have a strong, hyena-like laugh, which could be identified at great distance.

Bennett was in fourth grade when he first met John one spring afternoon in a vast, untouched tract of land that he walked through on his way home from school. Bennett called it the cornfield, although there wasn't a single stalk of corn in sight. Instead, there were dense clusters of oak trees and bushes, bird's-foot violets as blue as the sky, turtles and snakes, mysterious dirt trails that slithered into the trees.

Bennett had two favorite spots. One was a hill where the land dropped away and the wind blew with such constant force that you could sit with your eyes closed and imagine you were rushing through space as the earth spun on its axis. He would spend hours on that hill with a weed in his mouth, thinking and letting the time flow by with the wind. His other spot was a pond, green and dark and full of tadpoles in warm months. He liked to take off his shoes and walk in the mud flats, getting the dark ooze between his toes. He never went there without writing his initials in the mud. Several days later, the initials would be gone, dissolved in the slime, and he would write them again. He wanted some part of himself with the pond at all times.

One afternoon, he had just finished inscribing his initials in the flats when he heard a hyena laugh. It was John, who had secretly been watching him from underneath an oak tree, his arms folded on his chest. The other boy inspected Bennett's work, then proceeded to erect his own initials in the mud, out of sticks. He sharpened the sticks with his jackknife and drove them half a foot down into the mud. The pattern of vertical posts spelled J.L. Neat, Bennett said. The older boy folded up his knife with a click, stood back and admired his creation, then disappeared along one of the dirt paths.

John's initials remained standing all the way until summer, when the mud dried and cracked and finally heaved the sticks over.

The last day of school that first year, the boys almost burned down the cornfield. John decided that with summer coming on they would need protection from Indians. So the boys built a fort, in the corner of the cornfield nearest the Sears and Roebuck building. They made it from logs and large rocks. A fort naturally needed a campfire. Got any matches? asked Bennett. John got a pained look on his face and took out his magnifying glass, which produced a flame in just under three minutes. Almost immediately, however, the fire slipped out of control and spread to some dry brush. Oh my gosh, oh my gosh, oh my gosh, Bennett screamed and started running in circles. John immediately grabbed Bennett by the shoulders and pleaded, half-crying, Please don't tell my father. Oh my gosh, Bennett yelled, let's get help. There's a fire station over there, I'm going to tell them. And he started running wildly toward the edge of the cornfield, John weaving behind like the tail of a kite. They ran toward the Sears and Roebuck building, across Poplar Avenue, dodging the oncoming cars, and to the fire station on Belle Meade. You can't, wailed John, they'll know that we did it. They'll tell my father. Bennett didn't answer but kept running. He burst through the door of the station and shouted that there was a fire next to the Sears and Roebuck building. Then he bolted out and flew in the opposite direction of the cornfield, John following again. They didn't look behind them and they didn't stop running until they were nearly a mile away, near the Rexall, both of them panting and sweating. In a few minutes, they calmed down and sat in a clump of grass with their legs crossed under them, staring at each other in disbelief. Promise you won't tell my father, John said. I promise, said Bennett.


Afternoons, Bennett would drop over from school with some idea he'd read in *Popular Science* and find John stretched out and spindly on his bed, brooding over his most recent batch of poor grades. John's mind raced at ten thousand R.P.M.s, but the gears spun aimlessly without another good mind to engage. At the mention of a new project from Bennett, with the barest shred of description, he would perk up and roar into action, pulling electrical wires, resistors, soldering irons, or whatever he thought was required from boxes piled here and there around his room. Then, with a Bob Dylan song howling in the background, they'd get down to business. Over the years, the young scientists

built a walkie-talkie, a crystal radio, a thermostat, a tele-
scope from scratch with an automatic tracking device.
John never saved the directions that came with new
parts, he never drew up detailed schematic diagrams,
and his wiring would wander drunkenly over the circuit board. But he had the magic touch, and when he
sat down cross-legged on the floor of his room and
began fiddling, the transistors hummed. Loosey-goosey,
he would say matter-of-factly. It just needed some
loosey-goosey. Dumbfounded, Bennett would watch
over his friend's shoulder in an attempt to discover why
things worked better in John's room than his own, but
the attempt was totally useless, nor did John explain
anything. John didn't squander his time on theory.

Their most brilliant collaboration was a commu-
nication instrument that transmitted sound by light,
rather than by electrical impulses along wires. When
someone spoke into one end of the device, the sound vibrated a balloon, on which was mounted a bit of silvered glass. A beam of light reflected off this little mirror
across the room to a receiver. Because the mirror was
vibrating in response to the person's voice, the intensity
of reflected light also fluttered, precisely encoding the
most minute intonations of voice spoken by a skeptical
inquirer. The result was that the flickering light, gathered up at some distance away and processed through

another gadget, could be converted back to the original voice. It was miraculous. And it worked.

The first trial of their device had occurred on a rainy Saturday in April. They'd been lying on their backs for some time on John's floor, discussing what message should be communicated in the inaugural run. The air was sticky and the room had been darkened and the only light was the yellow transmitter beam, diagonal across the room.

It should be something immortal, said John, like: Once upon a midnight dreary, while I pondered, weak and weary. Bennett thoughtfully considered this proposal and shook his head no. How will we be regarded by posterity, he said, if our first message is poetry? Shouldn't we say something scientific, like the first ten digits of pi? I don't know, said John, scratching a mosquito bite. You got the tape recorder hooked up? Yep, said Bennett. The microphone was taped flush to the amplifier at the receiver. Bennett lifted his leg and pressed down the record button with a toe.

At that moment, John's father burst into the dim room, gave John a look sharp as hail, and shouted, Where are my socks, dammit? Have you been wearing my socks again?

John sagged visibly, but he didn't answer his father. Instead, he stood up, went to the tape recorder, and played it. At which point, all present heard the words, Where are my socks, dammit? Have you been wearing my socks again? the sentences having been faithfully conveyed across the room on a fluttering sliver of light. It works, he said.

John's father said nothing more and left immediately, certain that he'd been mocked. As soon as he'd gone, a dark wave came again over John and he sank to the floor. Why does he talk to me like that? he said, trying to hide his face. Sometimes I want to kill him.

Let's go for a walk, said Bennett. It's raining, said John. It's not raining hard, said Bennett, let's go. He lightly touched John's shoulder, and they went out the kitchen door and into the wet. Even in the rain, they could smell the sweet odor of the honeysuckles in bloom, entwined on the white wooden fences. They walked without words for a mile, just breathing in the honeysuckle air, until they were drenched. Finally, they stopped under a lamppost near John's house. It worked, Bennett said, and smiled. Yes, said John, it worked.

A month later, they entered their invention in the county science fair. The day before the judging of the fair, after numerous trial runs at up to fifty feet between talker and listener, something broke. No sound issued forth from the receiver. Even John was unable to discover what was wrong. Bennett went home in a terrible depression and wouldn't leave his room for the next twenty-four hours. A day later, John called, saying that he had carried their stricken contraption to the fair early in the morning and surreptitiously connected the transmitter to the receiver with a wire hidden under the table. Bennett gasped into the telephone. The judges had been fooled and awarded them first prize.

John's other passion was rock and roll. Over time, with funds from his grandparents, he had painstakingly constructed the finest high-fidelity stereophonic sound system in the city, right in his own room, with components bought through the mail from Heathkit. He had his own equipment for testing, and when parts didn't measure up, he would send them back with indignant notes: Dear Sir: What is happening in this day and age? Read the frequency specifications of your tweeter and compare to reality. Do you think you're dealing with some high school student? Bennett would read John's notes and admire his confidence and sometimes tell people at school that he was John Lerner's best friend.

Bennett also loved rock and roll and wanted nothing more than to throw on a Stones album and lie beneath the turntable suspended from the ceiling of

John's room. But not John. Having built the finest stereophonic system in the city, John had to hear the artists live. You have to watch their faces, Good Benito, he would say. But the sound is so much better on your system, Bennett protested. Why did you go to all that trouble? John didn't reply. You can't hear the high ranges in the clubs, Bennett pointed out correctly. We're going out, John said. And somehow, he convinced Bennett to sneak away with him after bedtime on schoolnights, against all regulations, to go downtown to Main Street and watch the faces of the musicians.

Bennett's bedroom was on the second floor of his house, at one end of a long hall. A storage room was at the other end. By good luck, the pecan tree draped over the roof outside his dormer bedroom window. On the nights of his clandestine excursions with John, he would wait a half-hour after the lights had blinked out downstairs, where his parents and brothers slept, and then creep out his window onto the roof and climb down to earth on the branches of that pecan tree, surprised and alarmed at his own boldness. John would be waiting for him at the bottom of the driveway, in the dark, and they would walk down the street and catch the Poplar bus downtown. They had to walk all the way to Poplar and Goodlett because the buses didn't run out to east Memphis in the evening. It always felt odd getting on that bus. They were the only white people, aside from the driver, and the blacks still sat bunched up in the back of the bus, even though the seating had been integrated by law for several years.

Downtown, the boys heard Jerry Lee Lewis sing Great Balls of Fire at the Club Paradise, Tommy Burke and the Counts do Stormy Weather at the Roaring Sixties, Rufus Thomas belt out Walking the Dog and Bear Cat. This was Memphis. Once in a while they heard Booker T. and the M.G.s. Booker T., who had a four-piece group, played the keyboards himself and looked more like a scholar than a musician. On occasion it was rhythm and blues, but mostly rock and roll.

Sometimes the boys got off the bus at midtown near the Poplar-Union Viaduct, at a coffeehouse called the Bitter Lemon, and took in the Guilloteens. The Guilloteens often sang early Beatles and Stones tunes, but they had the Memphis sound. And they had some tunes of their own, like I Don't Believe. They had a twelve-string guitar, a bass, and drums.

When the boys went to the Bitter Lemon, there was usually nowhere to sit, so they had to stand pressed against the glass window near the front. It was a tiny place not much larger than Bennett's bedroom, with only six or seven tables, and the music was so close and loud that you could see the Coca-Cola vibrating in your glass. But it was good rock and roll. John would wriggle around until he could see the musicians. Then, after the first set, he would close his eyes and just listen. Bennett did the same. In time, he understood about the faces.

Summers in Memphis, the air was so heavy and hot that when Bennett went outside for five minutes he felt like it was raining inside his clothes. A great many people wouldn't leave their air-conditioned houses for any reason while the sun was up. On the most humid days, Bennett and John rode their bicycles to McKellar Lake. McKellar flowed into the Mississippi, on the west side of Memphis. At that time, before the big chemical companies started dumping waste into the lake wholesale, McKellar was clean, and the two friends would strip to their underwear and swim out to a little island in the middle of the lake. Hey, Good Benito, let's race, John would say and leap into the lake, flailing his arms and sticking out his white, sunken chest. Bennett always got to the island first. He was much stronger than John. But everytime when the two boys got to the lake, John would challenge him again: Hey, Good Benito, let's race. Bennett loved him for that.

They would take sandwiches, wrapped in plastic

bags and strapped to their waists. After lunch, they would lie in the shade of a tree on the island. They never talked much as they lay in the shade of that maple underneath the thick summer air. Mostly, they quizzed each other on science facts. What's the circumference of the earth? Bennett would ask. Twenty-four thousand miles. What's the distance to the nearest star? John would ask. Twenty-four trillion miles. What's the coldest possible temperature? Two hundred seventy-three degrees below zero, centigrade. It was a universe of certainty and logic, and they basked in their knowledge.

They pledged to each other that for the rest of their lives, no matter where else they lived, they would remain friends, they would return together to that spot every summer, to lie under the maple and look at the white ridges and the water and feel the close Memphis heat.

Often they didn't say anything. They just lay under the shade of that maple tree, feeling secure. Occasionally, they would hear the faint voices of people on a passing sailboat, but the voices would soon fade and get swallowed in the dense summer air. The island was quiet like cotton, and hours went by as if time didn't exist.

•     •     •

## Good Benito

For a decade or so after they graduated and left Memphis, Bennett wrote to John twice a year. John seldom wrote back. Finally, Bennett stopped writing. He would sometimes hear about his friend through John's mother. John went to college in North Carolina, then lived in Los Angeles, Chicago, Palo Alto. He became an electrical engineer and started his own company and was a success. John lived his whole life in science. Bennett did as well, for a time.

**A**fter the rocket launch at the Galloway Golf Course, Bennett began to realize that he was
better suited for theory than for experiment. Bennett
pondered things. He was a ponderer. He wondered why
the sky turned red at the end of the day. He wondered
why soap bubbles formed in nearly perfect spheres, why
all snowflakes had six sides. He wondered why a spoon
halfway in water appeared to bend in two, why chalk
squeaked. He wondered why a spinning top didn't fall
over but instead slowly gyrated. He wondered why the
sun didn't burn up, whether outer space went on forever. He wondered why clouds formed high in the air
and not on the ground. He wondered how sap could

rise in trees, against gravity, what made rainbows, what made the dark lines on the surface when water was poured in a bowl. He wondered why upstairs was usually warmer than downstairs.

He lies on his bed in late afternoon. Why must a focusing mirror be parabolic in shape? Why won't a spherical or flat mirror work? Why? There is a logical reason. He must know what it is. Closing his eyes, he imagines various shapes, pictures the trajectories of light rays. Silvered glass curving. Angles. Rows of imaginary lines, perpendicular to the surface as it undulates through space. Bennett, what are you doing up there? Yellow and gold light rays careening at angles to the perpendiculars, reflecting at equal angles, heading back into space, polished glass flexing and curling. Bennett, you've been spending too much time in your room. Come down. Out of all possible shapes, one shape. A parabola, an arc such that each point is equally distant from a directrix and focus. The hypothetical light rays fly in and emerge, converge to a point, converge to a focus. Glass gently sweeping through space. He has to know why.

The world buckled at its knees when Bennett took his first algebra course. He was thirteen. The class began with word problems, verbal applications of the rules of arithmetic. Mary has three pennies. If she gives two pennies to her younger brother Henry, how many pennies will she have left? Sometime in October, the problems progressed to more thoughtful examples, like: Mary is six years older than Henry, and Henry's age is two thirds of Mary's. How old is Henry? These conundrums had to be solved by trial and error. Finally, Bennett was taught how to symbolize the unknowns of a problem with $x$'s and $y$'s and to display everything in equations. Using the rules of algebra, the unknowns could be solved for in one logical step. What started with a messy statement involving Mary and her kid brother Henry ended with a single, sleek equation.

Bennett wouldn't have been happy with no mention of Mary and Henry. That kind of problem was for the pure mathematician: Consider object A, which is six units greater than object B, whereas object B has a measure two thirds that of A. No, Bennett was a scientist, and he wanted to begin in the dirt and debris of the real physical world. But he took pleasure in sifting through that world, distilling it, cleansing and purifying it until he was left with a single mathematical equation of inescapable solution.

In his American history class, even after reading the book, the class would argue for days about why the

Civil War started. The teacher would argue as well, first giving one reason, then another, walking up and down between the desks, until finally Bennett concluded that no one on earth knew why the Civil War started. It was the same with English and social studies. But algebra was different. There was always an answer, clean as a new Franklin half-dollar. The rules of logic guaranteed an answer. And when you found the answer, there was no arguing about it. You were right, and everyone agreed you were right.

He remembered everything about that algebra class. Mrs. Dixon had gray and white hair, which she kept pinned in a vertical bun. She wore dresses with large colored flowers on them. The floor was linoleum and looked like a checkerboard, with black and white squares. Just inside the door, to the left, was a coatroom with brass hooks on the wall. When someone misbehaved in class, he was sentenced to the coatroom, where everyone would soon hear him trying on other people's coats. Above the middle of the blackboard sat a big red clock, like an eye, reminding the class of how many minutes remained. The desks had swivel tops with grooves to hold pencils. Mrs. Dixon demanded that each student keep a highly sharpened pencil in the groove at all times. The pupils were not permitted to get up from their desks for any reason, including the toilet, except to sharpen their pencils at the back of the room.

Bennett couldn't wait to discuss each new technique in higher mathematics with John after school. John would get impatient and say, Yeah, yeah, I know about that stuff, and then he would bring out some dissected squid's eye or an electrical circuit he was working on.

It is early morning, before breakfast. Bennett stands in his room in his pajamas, looking idly out the window at the Taglias' house next door. A cedar fence separates the two houses. Magnolias grow along the fence. But from his bedroom window, Bennett can see over the magnolias, over the fence, and watch the withered old man slowly walk down the driveway to pick up the morning paper. The old man, the grandfather, speaks no English. Sometimes he mutters to himself in Italian. He leans to the left as he walks, slowly lifts each foot as if it were stuck in the asphalt. He is a tiny, thin stick, and he limps slowly down the driveway each morning, beneath the maple trees, to fetch the paper. It is good weather today, but the old man goes in all weather. Bennett has watched him for years. This morning, he estimates the length of the driveway and clocks the old man's walk with his watch and calculates how long it would take him to walk to the moon.

Bennett's classmates hated word problems. Indeed, they hated math altogether, but they'd rather have a tooth filled than be forced to sit down and contemplate word problems. Bennett, on the other hand, placed word problems on a level with Florida's pecan pie. Word problems were delicious. He devoured them. He convinced the flabbergasted Mrs. Dixon to give him additional problems, beyond the assignments, and when she ran out of problems he created them himself. After school, when the other boys played basketball or loitered behind the Rexall drugstore to smoke and discuss girls, Bennett went home and up to his room to do word problems.

His mother would come out of her bedroom where she'd been resting, wearing her pale amber robe, and stand at the foot of the stairs. Bennett, what are you doing up there, she would call up to him, in a polite voice. Nothing, he'd answer. Then he'd hear some whispering and Marty or Philip would ascend halfway up the stairs and recite as he'd been told: Bennett, what are you doing in your room? Masturbating, Bennett would answer, don't come up. After a moment, his mother would call up again: Sammy Abrams is such a nice boy, and he's invited you over to play. I don't like Sammy

Abrams, Bennett would answer through his closed door. What about Michael Solmson? replied his mother, he's a lovely boy. I don't like Michael Solmson, Bennett would answer. Then, his mother again: You're selfish and you're going to grow up miserable, with no friends. Just like Uncle Maury.

Bennett didn't understand why his mother called him selfish for staying in his room. In those years, and for many years after, he was terribly confused by what people said. One fall, after his weekly allowance was reduced by twenty-five cents, his mother explained that since the family business was doing well, it was a good time to save money rather than spend it. On another occasion, Bennett's cousin Laura, in her early twenties, announced that she was breaking up with her boyfriend because she loved him too much. Could that be what she meant? Bennett learned to hide his confusion and just nod his head. Then he'd go to his room to do word problems. He thought everybody should learn how to do word problems.

One o'clock in the morning. Old man Taglia walks at this hour, unobserved, his house dark and asleep. He limps slowly in the moonlight. There is another light. He looks up to his left, toward the second-floor window.

*Che diavolo, ci risiamo,* he mutters, and continues down the driveway.

Bennett sits at his oak desk. They are so beautiful, the equations. Even visually beautiful, but especially beautiful in the mind. Their precision and power are beautiful, and as he begins to understand an equation, he gets the same feeling as seeing a moonrise over trees. In his mind, it is dark and still and then the tops of the trees on the far side of the bay begin to glow slightly, white and soft, and the white gets brighter, silhouetting the trees, and then a small piece of moon appears and the mathematics opens up and contains and shines in perfection. It is one in the morning, but he is not tired. He gains strength from himself. He does not need to go to the library, he does not need to ask other students or grown-ups for information or help. He can be here alone, in his room, with the beautiful mathematics and the moon and figure things out on his own. He can sit here naked at his oak desk with the clean, white paper and work in the absolute certainty and the solitude and perfection. Gliding through the world in his mind, he doesn't worry about his small height or his pimples or his problems with talking or his confusion at what people say. It is a world without bodies. It is a world of clear logic and grace. It is the best part of loneliness, without the sadness.

The real reason Uncle Maury was miserable was because he was always in hock. He had a gambling problem.

When he was in junior high school, in Nashville, Maury flipped coins with other boys during school recess. In high school, he played poker. Five card draw, with maximum bets of a dime. Even with the ten-cent maximum, he could win or lose ten dollars in a Saturday night. That was a lot of money for a skinny kid in the mid-1930s. He began betting on basketball games, dog races, political elections, anything that smelled of money and risk. After he was forced to leave college for borrowing and gambling away his tuition funds, he drifted from one job to another until his sister married Bennett's father. Then he moved to Memphis to be taken into the family business, a large retail clothing store started by Bennett's grandfather on his father's side.

Maury lived alone, in a rented duplex on West Galloway that Bennett's parents quietly paid for. He seldom went out. He dreaded leaving his house. He did, in fact, have a desk at the store office on Madison and Highland, and he drew a regular salary, but he rarely showed up to work.

Maury's salary didn't cover his expenses. Every few weeks, Bennett's mother got a letter from him asking for a loan. He lived only a couple of miles away, but to ask for money he used the mail. Bennett could recognize his uncle's back-slanted handwriting when he picked up the mail at the bottom of the driveway.

Maury invited his nephew over once a week, on Sunday afternoons, to figure out the odds for him. Sometimes it would be dog racing, sometimes a new kind of card game. Bennett rode his bicycle. They would clear off the clothes from the couch. Is your mother angry at me? Maury always asked when Bennett first arrived. Maury's face was as humble and honest as a freshly peeled fruit. No, Bennett answered. Maury

would let out a sigh and settle back in the couch, holding one hand on the top of his head to cover his bald
spot. Then he would tell stories. He would tell about
how his grandfather came over from Russia and got
robbed of his only pair of shoes on his first day in New
York City. He would tell about the various women he
had wanted to marry. Sometimes he would talk about
the lucrative Lang business, in the old days before his
time, when they had just two rooms on Parkway near
the Parkway Hotel and worked twelve hours a day sell-
ing hats and pants in their shirtsleeves. Maury had enormous admiration for Bennett's grandfather, a self-made
man who had opened the store by himself in 1934, a
man who always believed things would turn out in his
favor and who made things turn out in his favor. As
Maury recounted, when Bennett's grandfather would
come into a room, people could feel his success in the
air and would stop talking and just wait for him to say
something. The only thing Bennett knew about his
grandfather, besides Maury's stories, was the huge, oval
photograph of him in the living room.

Maury would tell stories a while, then pitch his
nephew a new problem in probability theory. Bennett
would calculate a while and give his uncle an answer.
Taking a deep breath, Maury would study the numbers,

nod his head gravely, and say, That's very interesting, Bennett, one can never be too careful in these matters, and the analytical forces at play are considerable.

As far as Bennett could tell, Maury never bet by the numbers. If he had, he couldn't have lost nearly as much and as fast as he did. But he always nodded seriously and said, That's very interesting, Bennett. Then he would stand up and make his way to the telephone across the room.

Maury's house was permanently stuffed with boxes, as if he were constantly in the process of moving. Boxes filled the rooms, the hallways, even the bathroom, stacked up to five and six feet high. Only a narrow, winding path between the boxes connected one room to another. Clothes draped over the boxes and chairs. The kitchen floor was submerged beneath a sea of green glass, empty Coke bottles, maybe a couple thousand, standing upright and covering every square inch of linoleum. But Maury didn't need his kitchen. He had pizzas delivered, as his drooping belly showed. He often started breathing heavily just walking up the three steps to his front door.

Maury would come back from the telephone looking hopeful, one hand protecting the bald spot, and sit down on the couch. Has that kid in study hall been making fun of you again? he would ask. Bennett shook his head no. Well, you tell me if he bothers you, said Maury. You tell me, okay? I'll fix his wagon. It's all right now, said Bennett. Good, said Maury, because I'll fix his wagon if he bothers you again. What are you learning about in science class? Cells, Bennett said. That's fine, said Maury, that's fine. Bennett nodded and smiled.

Maury would leave again and return with two Coca-Colas, somehow retrieved from the refrigerator, and they would sit and drink their Cokes and listen to Maury's old Zenith radio. After a while, Maury would ask Bennett again if his mother was angry at him. Bennett again said no. Then Maury would stand up and tell Bennett he had to go out and meet somebody.

**I**t is a hot evening in May, and Bennett lies on his bed in his pajamas. He reaches in a drawer of the bedside table and takes out the cigar box of photographs. The pictures are of his father, Sidney. Bennett knows them well. In the first, Sidney is about ten years old and stands on the front porch of a house with his mother and father. Sidney wears knickers and anxiously stares at a black spotted dog. In another, Sidney and Bennett's mother stroll on a beach. They are young, in their early twenties, before Bennett was born, and Sidney's chest is bare and he smiles and looks sure of himself and firmly holds his young bride's hand. In another,

Sidney is wearing his naval uniform. His hair is parted smartly, and the uniform fits well. In another, he sits on the edge of a bed, his hair tousled, playing a guitar.

Bennett holds each photo up to the bedside lamp, studies his father's expression, studies his eyes and his hands, but especially the eyes. Then he collects the photos and puts them back in the cigar box and the drawer.

Bennett doesn't know the man downstairs dressed up as his father. When Sidney comes in the front door after work, he mumbles hello, looking at the floor, and that is often the only word from his mouth for the evening. When he walks out of a room, he turns off the lights, regardless of whether a wife or a son is there reading or playing Monopoly or practicing the piano. He has his chair and his dinner and his bed. At Thanksgiving, when Bennett's uncles and aunts and cousins come to the house and crowd into the family room talking and laughing and drinking, Sidney quietly goes to the red Queen Anne chair in the corner, not his favorite chair but an adequate chair, and picks up his book and reads, as if the room were empty.

After many years, Bennett and his brothers have stopped seeing this man, just as he doesn't see them. When they pass him in a hall or momentarily occupy the same room, they no longer see him. But the man in the photographs is not invisible. Bennett's father is in the photographs.

As he puts the cigar box away, Bennett hears a car come for his mother, in the driveway below. It is Hubert Simon. Mr. Simon is taking Bennett's mother dancing at the Dixie Blue Club, one of the stops in the Cotton Carnival. The Carnival has been going four nights now. Bennett's mother goes out dancing every night during Cotton Carnival week, just as her mother did long ago. All through the year, she looks forward to that special week in May. She loves to dress up in the costumes and to dance and to see who is there. She doesn't even try to get Sidney to take her. Most years, she goes with Hubert Simon. How do you like my costume? she asks, swishing into the living room where Sidney sits in his chair. From his room upstairs, Bennett can hear her, can imagine what he doesn't hear. I think it's marvelous, she answers herself happily, and she walks over to the mirror in the entrance hall to fix up her hair. I hope I don't perspire, she drawls, and examines her underarms to see if she is already moist. I wonder what Betty is going to wear? Last year she came as a leopard. I wish you had seen her. That was her. That really was her. Bennett's mother continues to work on her hair. Then Hubert Simon's car comes up the driveway and honks once, politely, and waits with its lights on, illuminating the trunk of the pecan tree. Bennett's mother gives Sidney a kiss on the cheek and he smiles briefly and she leaves through the front door and into the heavy, warm air.

Bennett hears the car door open and close twice, and he turns out the lamp in his bedroom and wonders whether his mother misses Sidney when she goes out dancing and whether she is in love with Hubert Simon.

**N**o matter how exasperated Bennett's mother was with Uncle Maury, she asked him to come to dinner every couple of weeks. He always arrived with a large assortment of tools strapped around his waist—a hammer, screwdrivers, pliers, drill, chisels, bits, wrenches. Maury was a fixer, and when he came for dinner he insisted on fixing anything that was busted.

Bennett was Maury's assistant in these matters. He shared with his uncle the acute pleasure, even the urgency, of fixing things. In Maury's own house practically everything needed fixing. Lamps were permanently inoperative; the bathroom faucet squirted water over the basin; the stereo, when it was not at the pawn shop, played out of only one speaker. But when Maury arrived at Bennett's house, he was ready to fix things, and he did. He would stride slowly across the kitchen floor, his tools rattling heavily as he walked, and say to Bennett, Let's get 'em.

Florida gave Maury a wide berth. Once, he fixed the washing machine in such a way that he did away with the spin cycle, where the water is let out of the tub and the clothes are spun around at great speed. For several weeks, Florida had to wring out the clothes by hand before putting them in the dryer. Then she called a Maytag repairman. After the episode with the washing machine, whenever Maury came through the kitchen, Florida would place her considerable body between him and the appliances, her version of raising a cross in front of a vampire. The refrigerator's making that funny noise again, Maury would say to Florida and begin taking out one of his wrenches. You just go on right out of this kitchen, Mr. Maury, Florida would reply sternly, with her back against the refrigerator. You ain't studying this frigerator, and it ain't studying you.

After he'd been in the house scarcely ten minutes, Uncle Maury would start getting telephone calls. Evidently, his business associates knew whenever he made one of his rare outings from West Galloway and would call him as soon as he made a landing. Maury would interrupt his repair work to answer calls, writing down notes in the notebook he carried with him. During dinner, he would have Florida take messages for him, a nuisance she much preferred to having Maury himself invade the kitchen.

Despite the many tools that he carried attached to his body, Maury would usually not have the one tool he needed. But he had a genius for improvising. Bennett once saw him mend an electrical connection in the TV by melting solder with a hot poker from the fireplace. Another time he used his belt buckle to straighten out the chain in the flush mechanism of the guest toilet. He was terribly proud of his inventions. When he would get under a leaky sink or a toilet with some special home-made tool, he would say, Now we're going to town, aren't we, Bennett. Let's get 'em. Then he would forget about his bald spot and reach in with both hands.

It was left to Bennett to tell Uncle Maury what needed repair. For some reason that Bennett could not fathom, his uncle's small accomplishments seemed to irritate his mother. While Maury was at work with his tools, she would move from room to room with her phone calls or music or paperwork, vacating a room as soon as he entered it. One evening when Bennett was in the tenth grade, however, she was forced to acknowledge her brother's services. She was going out to a party, her hair dryer had suddenly broken, and she had no alternative but to ask Maury to fix it. His work was quick and well done. Good as new, Lenore, he announced loudly, smiling at Bennett and standing in front of his sister's closed door. She opened her bedroom door, barefoot and holding two pairs of shoes, and wordlessly accepted the hair dryer. A couple of weeks later, when Maury came over, she told him she'd prefer that he stop fixing things in her house. Maury hung his head, and she hesitated and then said he could fix things in the bomb shelter.

The bomb shelter. In the spring of 1962, Bennett had convinced his parents to build a fallout shelter. The president of the United States was coming on the television, pointing his finger straight into the family room and telling them to go out and build a bomb shelter. President Kennedy convinced Bennett. Bennett convinced his parents.

Everywhere Bennett went—in drugstores, in doctors' offices, at school—he saw copies of a government booklet called *Fallout Protection: What to Do About Nuclear Attack.* The booklet was blue and red and it had the national seal with the eagle on the cover. Magazines had pictures of cities with concentric circles centered on the downtown area, showing the level of destruction at various distances from the point of explosion of a nuclear bomb.

At Bennett's school they stocked the basement with canned food and water and lined the walls with large sandbags. The students were given instructions about what to do during an attack. First, stay away from windows. Get down on the floor under your desk with your hands over your head, and by no means look out the window or you'd be blinded by the flash. Then, after the initial blast, go to the basement.

Every month or so, the school would have a civil defense practice. A siren would go off and they would shout to each other, This is a test, this is a test, and drop to the floor and roll underneath their desks. A cheery, middle-aged woman named Mrs. Abernathy was in charge of civil defense at the school. She split her time between civil defense work and guidance counseling for the juniors and seniors.

Several boys in Bennett's eighth-grade science class made bets on when the nuclear war was going to start. One kid bet on three years, another on one year. A boy who had done a project on impurities in water bet four weeks' allowance that the bombs would start dropping within five months. Bennett stopped thinking about what he would be when he grew up. He stopped thinking about going to college, or even finishing high school. He was fourteen, and he believed that he would not live to be fifteen.

Bennett had nightmares about a nuclear attack. In one dream, he is riding his bicycle in the neighborhood when he looks up and sees a dark gray cylinder whoosh by overhead, like a shark. He can see its tail fins. It moves silently. This one missile goes by, headed for downtown Memphis, and he knows that it is a Russian nuclear missile and that in seconds the world will be over. He has a quick, nauseous feeling and the thought: So this is how the world ends. It couldn't be helped. In another dream, he is looking down at a city from the perspective of a bird. He sees tall buildings, windows reflecting sunlight, roads, a green park area. Suddenly the buildings flash bright red, then blinding white, then disappear altogether, vaporized. It all happens in silence. In another dream, he is in the school basement. It is packed with people. Everyone is throwing up. Among the fifty or sixty people, he recognizes his mother, his father, his brothers, Uncle Maury, his math teacher, his piano teacher, John, Rabbi Spear. No one seems to be noticing anyone else. They are all vomiting in their own corners, suffering alone. It is dark and it smells and he knows that everyone will soon die.

Bennett would wake up sick to his stomach and

still terrified after he'd turned on the lights. All of the dreams were soaked in a feeling of helplessness. Not just helplessness once the nuclear war had already started, but helplessness beforehand, in the inevitable slide of the world toward destruction. It was the feeling of help-lessness that Bennett hated most. He hated to be out of control. When he began reading about fallout shelters, he decided that here was a solution to the problem. A fallout shelter couldn't help if you lived near ground zero, but if you lived ten miles out, as the Langs did, it could save you from radiation death. For weeks at the dinner table, while his younger brothers sat mutely, Bennett pleaded with his parents to build a fallout shel-ter. He was so frightened that they finally agreed.

A company called Radpro built the shelter. Rad-pro hadn't been in business very long, but neither had any of the similar outfits that appeared suddenly at that time. Radpro came out with a bulldozer and removed 4,500 cubic feet of dirt from Bennett's backyard.

The construction lasted two months. Every day at seven in the morning the men came up the driveway in two red trucks. Each truck had a mushroom cloud with an X through it painted on the side and Triple Man in white letters on the front.

The shelter took up most of the backyard. The Langs had a red brick patio next to their back porch and behind that a quarter-acre out to the wooden fence bordering the neighbors' yards. The bomb shelter sat in the middle of that quarter-acre, between a yellow poplar and a sycamore. The swing set had to come down.

Once the project was under way, Florida would stand on the back porch with her hands on her hips, look at the giant hole in the backyard, and frown. Bennett, why Mr. and Miz Lang spendin' all their money on this thing? she said. It's a fallout shelter, Bennett answered. It will keep out the radiation if a nuclear bomb is dropped on Memphis. Florida stared at him, bewildered. She watched the men put in steel girders and pipes, repeated that Mr. and Miz Lang were wasting their money. Then she would start singing a gospel hymn and go back to her chores in the house.

The building took place over the summer, when Bennett was out of school. He got to know one of the men pretty well. His name was Pete. Pete was in his twenties, muscular, and didn't wear a shirt. He had a crew cut and two gold teeth. Pete let Bennett follow him around and watch what was going on. They don't pay us shit for this work, said Pete, but it's good experience. Pete's ambition was to build swimming pools. Pete had a girlfriend named Thelma who picked him up early in her blue Chevrolet on days when his boss wasn't there. You see that good-looking bitch who picks me up? Pete said to Bennett more than once. Bennett nodded. Shit, she's got some tits, don't she, Pete said. When Thelma drove up, she would get out of her car wearing a flimsy halter top, saunter slowly around the perimeter of the shelter so that the other men could see her, and then ride away with Pete.

In fact, Bennett did notice Thelma, but he was much more concerned with the air-filtering system. In his understanding of fallout shelters, the air-filtering system seemed the most crucial part. Death was most likely to come from the billions of radioactive particles floating in the atmosphere for weeks after the detonations of the bombs. A shelter could stock food and water for months, but not air. You had to get air from the outside. Consequently, you had to purify it.

Air was sucked into the shelter through three green air pipes sticking above the ground. The air pipes had conical metal hats, to prevent debris from falling in. Air was taken in through the undersides of the metal hats, then passed through a filter before entering the breathing space. A Geiger counter monitored the level of radiation inside the shelter and also outside, above ground. The roof of the shelter had three feet of dirt on top of it.

During the summer work, it was ferociously hot and the air was still and the men wore short pants. You could see the steam rising from their bodies when they poured water on their heads every half-hour. Bennett's mother asked Florida to make lemonade for the men. She herself never went outside while the work was in progress. Florida put the lemonade in a glass pitcher and set it on a white wrought-iron table on the brick patio. Every ten minutes or so, one of the men would walk over to the table, sweating furiously, and drink a whole glass of lemonade in one gulp. Shit, this is good lemonade, Pete said to Bennett. Tell your momma she makes good lemonade. Florida used up about two dozen lemons per day. She would stand at the kitchen counter squeezing lemons and mutter, Mr. and Miz Lang just wastin' their money.

The shelter was finished in September. Above ground all you could see was a mound of dirt rising up a foot and the three green air pipes poking up a little past that. The entrance was a lead-lined door lying flush against the ground. Beneath the door was a steep stair-case going down. Bennett's parents provisioned the shelter with five bunk beds, canned tuna fish, canned vegetables, peanut butter, saltine crackers, boxes of cookies, 200 gallons of water, two first-aid kits, tools, flashlights, a radio, toilet paper, two portable toilets, playing cards, and a game of Monopoly. It was better built and equipped than the shelter at school and, for the next several years, Bennett rehearsed in his mind how he would escape and run home to his own shelter if an attack came during school hours.

One day when the shelter was almost finished, Pete said to Bennett, You gettin' a gun? What do you mean? Bennett answered. Shit, a gun to keep your neighbors out, said Pete. Your neighbors been watching this thing going up, and you know goddamned well that they're going to be stampeding that door like a bunch of bulls when the fireworks start. That lock's not going to keep them out. I'd get myself a gun if I was you. Goddamned right, I'd get myself a gun, a .38-caliber Colt revolver is what I'd get. It has good stopping power. Bennett listened to Pete and tried to imagine Mr. and Mrs. Davies and their three children standing outside the door of the shelter and Sidney standing inside with a gun. He couldn't decide what came next. They never got a gun for the shelter. But Bennett worried about what Pete said.

When the shelter was finished, Bennett was so relieved that he let Marty and Philip rampage alone in his laboratory for a whole Saturday morning. He figured that was payment for something, or maybe his thanks to God for saving him and his family. The next day, he walked around and around that precious mound of dirt, admiring it from all sides. Then he went down inside and rearranged the cans of tuna fish and tested the radio and the Geiger counter and lay on a bunk bed.

When the Cuban Missile Crisis arrived a month later, Bennett was not frightened. In fact, he was pleased. He had always believed, in some deep, secret cave within himself, that he could solve any problem with a reasoned approach. He was ready for the bombs to start falling.

The only use any of the Langs got out of their bomb shelter was about six or seven years later, when Marty stealthily took his girlfriends down there for romantic purposes. By then the place was already smelling of mildew. Slowly, it filled up with water. On a trip home right after college, Bennett opened the lead-lined door and peered down with a flashlight and saw four feet of water and loose boxes of crackers floating everywhere. Bennett's parents hired a man to drain the shelter, and he did, but he said it wasn't built well and would fill up with water again. Around 1980, Bennett's parents dug up the whole thing and replaced it with a swimming pool.

**T**here were thirty-five kids in Bennett's confirmation class at Temple Isaiah. His mother knew the names of all the young women in the class and would go down the list every time a Pi Gamma Pi dance loomed on the horizon. Lisa Adler. Kathy Silverstein. Susan Shapiro. Bennett would always remember those girls, not from sitting in class with them for thirty Saturdays in a row, but from hearing their names read out by his mother like stock market quotations.

He found it incredible that out of the five thousand girls of his age in Memphis, a number he had carefully estimated, only nineteen were qualified to consort with him. He resisted. He never went out with any of the girls in his confirmation class, except once, on a night that the rain came down in buckets. It was a double date. Bennett's girl was a smoker and kept offering him a cigarette. When it became apparent that he wasn't going to join her in smoking, she lost interest in him for the rest of the evening and busied herself with small items in her purse. The boy who drove, Herbert Stearn, wore exceptionally thick eyeglasses. Herbert could barely see in strong daylight, under clear skies. On the way home, Bennett had to get out of the car every few blocks in the pouring rain and walk up to street signs to figure out where they were.

Bennett was fifteen when he began his confirmation classes. At first, he resented surrendering his Saturday mornings to religion. But his parents told him he had to do it. John had done it.

Unexpectedly, Bennett became friends with the rabbi. Rabbi Spear was a short, stubby man, and he looked like a bulldog, but he spoke in a soft, quiet voice, and he made you want to talk to him. The rabbi would often invite Bennett to his study after class. He would first excuse himself so that he could go to the office to take off his black robe; he never put on or took off his robe in front of anybody. A minute later he would return to the study, smiling apologetically, and ask Bennett to sit down in the chair near his desk.

## Good Benito

Rabbi Spear would sit behind his desk with his elbows propped up, and Bennett would suddenly find himself telling the rabbi things that he didn't tell anyone else. He told him about his difficulties with girls. Bennett couldn't talk to John about girls because John didn't know anything about girls. Florida sometimes helped, with her unspoken signals, but Florida was a female, after all, and there were things he couldn't ask her about. Like what to do when Lucia Barbee quickly stuffed her hands in her pockets after Bennett simply put his hand on top of hers at the Overton Zoo. Do you think I did something wrong? Bennett asked, barely getting the words out. Is there anything wrong with me? The rabbi, squirming a little in his undersized herringbone jacket, walked around his desk and put his hand on Bennett's shoulder. No, Bennett, he said softly, you didn't do anything wrong. What you did was perfectly natural. I shouldn't have done it, said Bennett. She probably thought . . . You didn't do anything wrong, said the rabbi. You've got a wonderful mind, remember that.

Rabbi Spear's study had a dark oak floor and blue enameled lamps and, on the wall behind the desk, a picture of a dinosaur, highly detailed and delicate. It was a drawing by the rabbi's son, who had died in a car crash. Other than that drawing, the walls were covered with books, on every imaginable subject. One by one, Bennett borrowed Aristotle, Maimonides, Kant, Thoreau, Kafka to take home to his living room, where Sidney sat silently in the evenings.

One Saturday after confirmation class, Bennett asked the rabbi about the .38 pistol and the bomb shelter. What was the right thing to do? The rabbi listened carefully, cradling his jaw with his hand and nodding slowly. After some moments he said, Yours is a most profound dilemma, Bennett. Most profound. There are times we must kill others to protect ourselves and our families, as in war. But your neighbors are not criminals, and they are not trying to harm you. They are trying to protect their own families. Yet your shelter is equipped for only one family.

The rabbi held a match to his pipe with his gnarled, stubby fingers, then continued. The right to survive is perhaps yours, since you built the shelter. On the other hand, why did you build a shelter and not them? Your neighbors might have lacked the money. And money is not always distributed fairly. Bennett nodded. Rabbi Spear wrinkled up his mouth. I'm afraid I cannot say what's right or what's wrong in this case, Bennett. That's sometimes the way. But I can say that it would be an awful thing to turn a gun on a neighbor. An awful thing.

Bennett sighed. What attracted him about Judaism was its belief in rationality. Rabbi Spear's reasoning seemed rational, but it didn't lead to an answer. Maybe that's what we need God for, Bennett said, to tell us what's right and what's wrong in the hard cases. We can figure out the rest by ourselves. Rabbi Spear released a mouthful of smoke, looked out the window onto Union, and replied, God needs man as much as man needs God.

Bennett sat there speechless, turning the rabbi's brilliant phrase over in his mind as if he were handling one of the precious books in his library. Did the rabbi mean that God is an invention of man? No, how could a rabbi say that God didn't exist on his own. But what could God need from man? Worship? Could God be that vain and insecure? Perhaps God needed man to help say what God was. But wouldn't that mean God had no qualities of his own, no absolute qualities? This possibility much disturbed Bennett. He wanted to believe that somewhere in the world there were absolute facts. Wasn't absolute cold two hundred seventy-three degrees below zero, centigrade?

Rabbi Spear got up from his desk and pulled a book from his shelves. It was *The Guide for the Perplexed* by

Moses Maimonides. Years later, that was the first book Bennett unpacked from the many boxes of books he received from the rabbi's estate. The rabbi had willed his entire library to him.

Temple Isaiah was an orange brick building on the corner of Union and Belvedere. It had a row of poplar trees along one side of the building. The confirmation classes were held on the third floor of the old building, looking out on Belvedere. Adjoining the main building was the great white dome of the sanctuary. Bennett liked the sanctuary. He liked the stately golden pipes of the organ, and the music. Almost all the songs were in Hebrew, which he didn't understand very well and so wasn't distracted. He could just lean back in his seat, listen to the beautiful music, and let his eyes run along the curved lines of the brass organ pipes.

Judaism for Bennett was that music, and his conversations with Rabbi Spear. He was proud of Jewish perseverance throughout history, but he didn't like the "us versus them" attitude of his Aunt Sadie. He wanted to be part of the world. He knew what he liked about being Jewish. He liked the ideas and the stubbornness and the successes. He liked it that Einstein and Freud and Gershwin were Jewish.

## Good Benito

Some of the other boys in the confirmation class were already sixteen, the sacred age when the law said they could wheel around the streets in their parents' cars. Bennett would sometimes drive with them to temple on Saturday mornings. After class, they would all go to lunch at the Pig-N-Whistle, on Union Street. The Pig served great onion rings and barbecue. The Pig didn't look like other restaurants. It looked like an English pub, except for its drive-in parking lot, where customers could eat in their cars. That's what the boys did. Once ensconced in an automobile, without an adult, they vacated the vehicle as little as possible. They would drive up to the Pig and a waiter in a white jacket would come out to the car to take their orders. What y'all want today? the waiter would say with a grin on his face. Plenty of napkins, the boys would answer and make slurping sounds like pigs feeding at a trough. If there were girls in a nearby car, they would slurp especially loudly. They always said they would send the white-jacketed waiter back to the kitchen immediately if the barbecue wasn't done to perfection. But it was always done to perfection. They drank root beer along with the onion rings and the barbecue. The Pig-N-Whistle was the other thing Bennett liked about being Jewish.

During confirmation class, Rabbi Spear would

sometimes try out a new idea of his own, pacing back and forth with his black robes flying and putting his heart into it. One day, he talked about his theory of happiness. He proposed that human feelings respond only to contrast and change, not to constancy, just as eyesight responds to contrasts of light and dark and to movement. The rabbi speculated that if emotions are similar to eyesight and other senses, then perhaps emotions were developed by nature as a survival mechanism.

Most of the kids in the class didn't pay much attention to the rabbi, whatever he talked about. They doodled in their notebooks and looked at their watches every ten minutes. This made Bennett angry. How could they not listen to a man who had helped desegregate the movie houses in Memphis? Didn't they see that Rabbi Spear thought of his students as his own children?

Long after he left Memphis, whenever Bennett returned for a visit he would go to see Rabbi Spear in his study. It was there that the rabbi met Bennett's fiancée, Penny, over the shocked objections of Bennett's mother. Penny was the daughter of a Methodist high school teacher in Pittsburgh. At that first meeting, the rabbi smiled at

Penny and asked her if she wanted to become Jewish. She looked at Bennett and down at the floor and said yes.

The subsequent conversion discussion took place in the conference room of the Holiday Inn on Summer Avenue, an unusual location chosen by Penny. Rabbi Spear didn't like this arrangement but he went along as a favor to Bennett. They were scheduled in the room from eleven to twelve. It was a very hot day in July. Outside, in the sweltering bright heat, the parched flowers drooped and even the squirrels hardly moved, their tails hanging limp. Inside, the air conditioners groaned. The future bride and groom and the rabbi sat bunched up at one end of a long table, all sweating. Rabbi Spear, now in his seventies, had begun having trouble with his legs, and a brown cane walker stood next to his satchel. He was not doing well in the heat. He had loosened his tie and taken off his jacket. He talked to Penny a few minutes, gave her several books to read, held her hand.

The next morning, he left a message for Bennett to meet him alone in his study. Bennett told Penny that he was going to visit a friend and drove down to Temple Isaiah and waited anxiously in the study while the rabbi finished some business. An overhead fan sounded like rapid breathing. In a few minutes, the rabbi limped into the room and moved slowly to where Bennett was sitting. He rested his hand on Bennett's shoulder. Do you love her? he asked quietly. Bennett did love her, completely. The rabbi could see that, and he sighed and affectionately touched Bennett on the head and gave him his blessing.

**P**enny was the second woman Bennett fell in love with. The first was Leila Phelps. Leila was his high school drama teacher.

Leila had graduated from the drama department of Memphis State University, gotten a teaching certificate, spent a couple of years in theater companies in Mississippi and Arkansas, a couple of years teaching high school in Arkansas. She had also acted in a summer stock company in New Hampshire, where she'd been told that she wouldn't go anywhere in theater until she eliminated her southern accent. She passed this bit of advice on to her students. Bennett had to endure countless pronunciation drills in her classroom where they would practice saying eye instead of ah and pen instead of pin. Leila hated discipline as much as her students did, and she visibly bit her tongue while they droned on for hours, but she fervently hoped that some of them would become actors and actresses. Leila was an optimist. In actual fact, none of her students had any aspirations for the stage. Bennett, for one, signed up for her course only because he needed an arts credit to graduate.

Each of Leila's students had to take a part in one of the school plays she directed. That's where the real teaching occurred. The rehearsals were after school, in the auditorium. School was out at 3:15 and play rehearsals began at 3:30. For rehearsals, Leila changed from her dress and high heels to blue jeans and tennis shoes. Her students called her Leila during rehearsals.

She had brownish red hair that always looked like she had just come from the shower and dried it roughly with a towel. She had green eyes that sparkled when she smiled. And she was always in motion. In the classroom, on the rare occasions she sat in her chair, she would continually rise and fall behind her desk, as if she were tightening and untightening her buttocks. More commonly, she was up on her feet, bounding about the room. When Leila moved, she moved with the grace of a dancer. She was completely unselfconscious about her body. During play rehearsals, when she would demonstrate how to walk or how to hold a particular pose, her body knew exactly what to do. She would attempt to sit still in the front row, watching her students, and suddenly leap to the stage. Like this, she would say, and her body, which had just been a leopard's in flight, would become a frantic child's or a wounded lover's. She needed no lines. Her body told the story.

Leila never worried about whether her students got the words right. She was concerned only with how they delivered the words. In addition to eradicating their southern accents, her mission was to teach them that meaning was conveyed not by what was said, but by the way it was said. From her seat in the front row, she would run her finger across her neck, signaling a halt, then mimic a badly delivered line. Then she repeated it three different times with three different rhythms and inflections. After each, she would ask for the intent of the speaker.

Bennett didn't understand Leila's approach to dialogue. He had frequent arguments with her during rehearsal breaks, when they would sit together on the steps outside the auditorium while the other kids walked to the Rexall for a soda or a smoke. Why have words if they're not to communicate? Bennett asked her one day, after staying up half the night memorizing his lines for *The Hasty Heart.* Putting her hands on her hips, Leila answered, Words are just indications. Words don't tell how someone is feeling. What about the Constitution? Bennett rebutted. In fact, he'd never read the Constitution, but he sensed that he was on solid ground. The Founding Fathers were presenting ideas, not emotions, he continued, and they worked hard to find the right words to say what they wanted. Leila studied Bennett's face for a moment, put an arm lightly around him, and said, Is Lachie reciting the Constitution to Margaret, or is he trying to tell her he loves her? That's ridiculous, Leila, Bennett answered. Whatever Lachie wants to say to Margaret, he can say it with words. If he wants to tell her he loves her, he can just say, I love you. Leila immediately dropped down two steps, looked up at Bennett, and said, in a bizarre, squeaky voice, Bennett, I love you. Please believe me, I love you. Do you believe me?

Something about this little performance cut Bennett up inside, but he didn't know what it was. A week later, at rehearsal, he had a scene where he was supposed to kiss Margaret. He'd done very little kissing in his life, and the girl who played Margaret wasn't much help. In the many rehearsals of that kiss, Leila gave such detailed instructions to Bennett that he eventually felt that he was kissing her instead of his classmate. After that, he couldn't look at her without feeling his face heat up and his legs go weak.

Bennett wanted to spend as much time with Leila as he could. But so did a lot of other students. She was generous with her time. She gave countless hours to small groups of students, going over and over scenes from the plays. Here, someone didn't act angry enough. There, someone stood stiffly. Here, someone needed to wait one more beat between lines. She would take a single student aside and work with her for half an hour while everyone else waited. She paid no attention to time. When 5:30 came, someone would have to tell her. When a student needed more work, she came to the auditorium on weekends.

Leila liked to paint, not fine arts painting but housepainting. She was good at it, and the school hired her to paint a new classroom. By this time, Bennett was taking every opportunity to be near her. He went to watch while she painted. It was a Saturday. She wore her theater clothes, her blue jeans and tennis shoes. She was painting a wall and stood on a ladder. Bennett stationed himself outside the classroom window and watched. Her brushstrokes were long and slow and rhythmic. Every few strokes, she would stop, reach over and dip her brush into the paint, then continue, all in one motion. She put the paint on thickly. It was so thick that Bennett could hear it spread over the wall. Then she would smooth it out evenly and perfectly. Her face and her hands gradually became covered with paint, but she didn't seem to notice. She was entranced with the feel of the paint and the sinewy motion, back and forth, back and forth, back and forth. Bennett watched her, unseen, for two hours.

Bennett would never have said anything remotely romantic to his drama teacher, and his passion would have quietly and desperately extinguished itself, but she began showing an unusual interest in him. She would append small personal comments to her greetings when they passed in the hall: I like that shirt you're wearing today, Bennett, or, You look a little tired today, Bennett. Were you out late last night? Or, You have a cut on your hand. Are you all right? She began gazing at him oddly in play rehearsals. She stopped sitting next to him on the steps during break.

One day in April, after class, she invited Bennett to come to her house after school to practice for the play. Bennett was so shocked that he stood in the hall long after his next class started, stood and stared at the slip of paper with her address on it, expecting it to disintegrate.

She lived in an apartment building on Seville Drive, near Summer and Perkins. On the front grounds sprawled a large swimming pool, still covered for winter. The building was yellow stucco, with white columns at each of the four entrances. Swirls of stucco stood out from the walls, like giant brushstrokes of paint. She lived on the third floor. An aging wood staircase led up to her door, the only door on that landing.

Bennett leaned his bicycle against the stucco wall, walked up the stairs. The stairs creaked. He was afraid someone would see him. He was about to explode. Did she understand what she was doing, the way that he felt? He stood outside the door a long time, shaking, before he knocked. She opened the door, then sat on the couch looking at him. Sitting down was out of the question. He stood by the door, paralyzed. Then she walked over to him, very close, found his hand, and kissed it. Then she put his hand on her breast.

He began going to her apartment twice a week. He told his mother he was visiting John.

She made him swear that he loved her. A hundred times he told her he loved her. She held him so tightly that her arms left red stripes on his back. Her fingernails left cuts on his chest. She scratched and she bit, but he never felt any pain. He wanted everything that she had. He was horrified about what was happening, but he found that he had no control over himself. At home, alone in his room with the door closed, he would sometimes take off his shirt and scratch his chest until the blood flowed and imagine it was her. He became more quiet than usual and he didn't understand anything and he thought only of her every night as he lay in his bed and stared at the twisted shadow of the pecan tree outside his window.

At the end of each visit, as the light through the blue shade started to fade, she wouldn't let him get up from her bed until he told her he loved her. He was happy to do so. He wanted to do so.

During those afternoon visits, they did spend a little time working on theater. They had the same arguments, only now far more personal. She would go through the same scene using different words every time. Her deliveries were brilliant, but her unconcern with the text drove him crazy. That's not what it says in the book, he would say angrily. Can't you read? Loosen up, Bennett, she replied, you're too goddamned literal and precise. You're probably going to be a lawyer or something. A scientist, he said. All right, she returned, you're going to be a goddamned scientist. Shit on your precision. You don't get it. It's you who doesn't get it, he shouted back. When he went home, he was sick that he had argued with her.

Uncle Maury was the only person Bennett ever told about Leila. Jesus, Maury said loudly. Bennett, my boy, he said putting his arm around him, you're growing up. But your high school teacher. Jesus, Bennett. How old is she? I don't know, said Bennett, maybe twenty-six. Jesus, said Maury, tell me about her.

Bennett tried to describe Leila, but he couldn't. Then Maury launched into a story about the first time he was in love. It was in Nashville, in his early twenties. The war was on, but Maury had been turned down for service. He met her in Centennial Park, on a Sunday in June. She had on a white cotton dress. He had some money, and they spent that summer and fall on riverboats, on picnics, taking drives. As he told the story, his eyes became teary.

What are you going to do? Maury finally asked. What was he going to do? Bennett had never thought about what Leila and he were going to do. He just assumed he would keep going to her apartment twice a week.

Maury went to the bathroom and came back with his trousers wet from the leaky faucet that sprayed over the sink. Got to go, said Bennett. Maury nodded and patted him on the back. Jesus, Bennett, he said, it's something, isn't it. You take care of yourself.

School was out in June. Bennett kept visiting Leila. Sometimes, he would go in the evenings, and they would swim in the pool, just the two of them, and watch the moon ride over the edge of the building. They went to places in south Memphis, where they wouldn't meet anyone they knew, little hamburger spots on Shelby Drive with blinking neon signs in front. They walked in Chandler Park, sat on the white enamel benches, hot to the skin even in the shade. One evening, they drove to the airport, stood by a fence, and looked at the planes going out one by one. They could just make out the thin row of heads. Then they played games guessing where the passengers were going and why, making up life stories for each tiny head. They went to McKellar Lake, early in the morning when no one was there, and swam out to the island where he and John used to go. Being there with Leila made him feel like he'd never been there before.

Bennett was leaving for college in September. One day in mid-August, Leila told him she was moving to New York. She wanted to try out for off-Broadway shows. She would send him her address and telephone number as soon as she got there. He was happy about this sudden announcement. He was going to college in the Northeast, and New York would be nearer than Memphis.

A few days later, when he went to visit her, the apartment was empty. No one knew where Leila had gone.

Many times over the following few years he called information in New York to find her, but she wasn't listed. Twice he went there himself to inquire at the off-Broadway houses. She wasn't there. Years later, he often wondered why the love of a seventeen-year-old kid should have meant anything to her.

**D**uring that last summer in Memphis, Bennett's mother was aware that something had happened to her son. One afternoon, she asked him to come into her bedroom and talk to her.

Bennett had sat by her bed many times. She often asked him to keep her company in the long afternoons as she rested in her bed, trying to recover from her last sleepless night. In recent years, he had not come so often, occupied instead in his own room upstairs.

She had made her bedroom emphatically feminine and round. The curtains were a soft, floral chintz, and a delicate cherry writing table stood next to her bureau.

111

**Good Benito**

Come, sit by me, she said, as he walked in. The room was dimly lit by the light from the bathroom, and the air conditioner softly hummed. She was lying on her side, wearing her pale amber robe, her eyes closed. I've been worried about you, Bennett, she said, still keeping her eyes shut. Is anything the matter? Nothing's the matter, said Bennett from the cushioned chair by her bed. We haven't talked for a long time, she said. You don't seem like yourself. He didn't say anything. You must be nervous about college, she said. A little, he said, shrugging his shoulders. She opened her eyes and turned over and looked at her eldest son. Is it a girl? He didn't answer, but he shifted in his chair. Oh, honey, talk to me, she said. I'm your mother. Talk to me. You're going away soon. Talk to me. Is she Jewish? Bennett didn't say anything. There was a long silence, and she looked up at the ceiling and then back at her son. She looked straight into him, with a look of exhaustion and sadness and love, and Bennett decided that she probably knew everything about Leila. Finally, she reached out for his hand and said, It doesn't matter if she's not Jewish.

**B**ennett is home for a weekend, in his old room upstairs. The bedspread is now soft blue silk. On a bureau, photographs of himself and his brothers, their wives, and their children. On his desk, near the window, an impatiens in a terra-cotta pot. The plant spills over the sides, its flowers salmon, translucent in sunlight. Each flower has five fragile petals, a tiny bud in the middle. He sits on the floor, his back against the knotted pine wall. His back hurts from carrying his suitcase up the stairs. Somewhere, the house creaks, then is silent again. He sits on the floor, rubbing his sore back, and suddenly bursts into tears. He doesn't know why.

**I**t's time we paddled up to Vassar, announced Bill. Bill was Bennett's college lab partner. They'd worked together through science courses since freshman year. Now they were juniors, they were physics majors, it was spring, and they were restless. Let's paddle up to Vassar, Bill said in the dining hall one day. It was Friday afternoon. They got into Bill's rusting Volkswagen and headed west on Interstate 84 for Poughkeepsie. Bill had arranged dates in advance.

Bennett liked Bill's company. But he was puzzled why they remained lab partners. Neither of them was much good in the laboratory. Bennett's experiments always had some mysterious little thing wrong. When he set up an experiment to measure Newton's gravitational constant, a tiny fiber twisted more than it should have, defying mathematical analysis. When he built an electronic device designed to light up when pure tones were offered it, his gadget caught fire at the first note. Bill had different problems. He overslept. He stayed up all night watching Humphrey Bogart movies, missed morning classes, and arrived at the lab half asleep. He would shuffle in through the heavy steel door, peer at Bennett's preliminary efforts, and say, The problems of two little people and an oscilloscope don't amount to a hill of beans in this crazy world. Then he'd propose that they leave the laboratory at once and retire to the Queen's Inn for pizza and beer. Bennett would nervously agree. He didn't like to abandon a project, especially one going poorly, but he'd already decided his forte was theory.

What time we meeting them? Bennett asked. They'd stopped in Danbury, Connecticut, for gas, one hour out on the road. Seven, at their dorm, Bill answered. You know where it is? Bennett asked. Bill looked offended. Where are we spending the night? Bennett asked. Bill glanced in the mirror and said, If we act suave, the ladies will invite us into their rooms for the night. Are you suave? I'm not sure about this whole thing, Bennett said. Here, said Bill, and he handed

Bennett the reefer he'd been smoking. Bennett took one drag and gave it back.

Bill may have been able to act suave, but he didn't look suave. His face was peppered with a three-day-old beard, and his sideburns plunged down to the bottom of his jaw. He wore his usual raggy jeans and his red Moroccan bedroom slippers. His wire-frame glasses were possibly suave.

They got to Vassar at seven and waited. The girls didn't show. This is real life, said Bill. They waited until eight and then went to a hamburger place near the college. Two couples came in, sat down at a neighboring table, and began laughing hysterically.

After the burgers, the boys drove about ten miles south of Poughkeepsie and pulled over to the side of the road for the night. They parked on a rise with a generous view of the Hudson. The sky was clear. On the other side of the river, about a half-mile away, lights flickered like lightning bugs in a dusty hedge. Occasionally, a ferry would drift slowly down the river, a green light on its starboard, a red on its port. Bill produced more marijuana from his glove compartment and began smoking heavily. They looked at the river. They ate a bag of chocolate-chip cookies. Suddenly Bill shouted, I've got it! We forgot to acoustically isolate the torsion balance. Presently he slumped over and fell asleep. Bennett climbed into the back seat. That was his last trip to Vassar.

The young men had actually forgotten their other mission to Vassar: to search for the nude photos taken of their freshman class at Blaine. They were certain that the photos were now in the hands of some all-women's college, like Vassar. They cringed every time they thought of those pictures and how they had lined up like sheep with their classmates, taken off their clothes as instructed, and been photographed front and back in the buff. It happened during freshman orientation week, as they were herded through the infirmary. A man wearing a tie and a look of importance had told them all that he was conducting sociological research on the relation between college performance and body type. So they stood in line, and each of the 600 of them, without a single refusal, stripped for one of the cameras. It was 1966. About a year later, the two boys were walking back from the library one evening, around midnight, when Bill suddenly slapped himself on the forehead and said, Holy shit, we were photographed nude. We let those bastards take naked pictures of us.

Bennett met Bill during a freshman physics course. One day during class, the students were calculating the speed of a projectile shot from the earth at a certain initial velocity and having attained a certain height. Bill came up with the correct answer immediately. Can you show us your calculation at the board, Mr. Prudhomme? said the professor darkly. Bill went to the blackboard and quickly scribbled two short equations. I used conservation of energy, he said, shrugging his shoulders. The professor looked annoyed and said, You're supposed to integrate the gravitational force along the trajectory. We're not doing conservation of energy in this chapter. Bill replied, The force method takes longer. Conservation of energy is the best way to handle this particular problem. With that, Bill brushed the chalk dust off his hands, strode back to his seat, and began reading an unauthorized copy of *Quantum Mechanics,* by Dicke and Witke.

Bill didn't wear a black armband to protest the Vietnam War, like other students did. He didn't go to the Student Union to hurl bananas at the secretary of state. Instead, he found his own issues. For one, he constantly denounced the fast, regimented pace of modern society. In his opinion, the source of most modern problems could be traced to the thoughtless hurry of ordinary life. Bill's mind worked fast, but he took his time in everything else. To emphasize his position, he wore bedroom slippers everywhere.

One Sunday in the spring of their sophomore year, as the boys lounged in Bill's dorm suite perusing the newspaper, Bill came upon a tiny article tucked away on page thirty-seven, like a preserved piece of ginger. It said that astronomers had just found evidence that the universe was two billion years older than previously thought. Here we have it, shrieked Bill, still in his pajamas. The cosmic breathing space to put things in perspective. This changes everything. Bennett looked up, dazed, from more urgent sections of the paper. But why is this important discovery on page thirty-seven? said Bill angrily. No one will have time to read that far.

*C'est vrai,* sighed Stuart, Bill's roommate and another of his admirers. Stuart was so skinny that his clothes seemed to move around by remote control. He was wearing a poisonous yellow tie and lay sprawled on his back on the couch. Do you know how few people take the time to read books these days? continued Stuart. Only one in a hundred reads more than two books a year. Source, demanded Bill. *Vanguard* magazine, said Stuart, pleased with himself. You should be reading books, not magazines, said Bill. Stuart winced. Magazines have facts, Stuart said defensively. Facts! shouted Bill, Yes indeed, facts. But who knows the facts? People believe in a world that is partly the world as it is and partly a world that they'd like it to be. Nobody knows the difference. That's why we need science. *Exactement,* Stuart said, and stopped there this time.

Stuart was another physics major. But he was not a member of the physics elite. Bennett and Bill were. At an early stage of their college career, they had been taken under the wing of a renegade assistant professor of physics named Harvey Galvinston. Galvinston had had some undisclosed altercation with the administration and decided to set up a mini-department under his personal direction. He secured a large empty room in the basement of the physics building, put five desks in there, for himself and four undergraduates, and declared his private college in session. No graduate students allowed. There was a blackboard, several bookcases, and a glaring fluorescent light on the ceiling. It was all well below ground level.

Galvinston selected his disciples by their performance on a single question: If a frictionless bug is sliding clockwise around the frictionless rim of a clock, starting at the twelve o'clock position, at what hour mark will the bug fall off? It was a perfect question for a budding theoretical physicist. Whenever a vacancy occurred among the four desks in his underworld domain, Galvinston would prowl around the physics classes and furtively deliver his bug problem to any new physics student who would receive it. Bennett and Bill both passed the test.

Once admitted to a desk in the basement, Galvinston's students got treated to advanced tutorials on all branches of physics. This was all extra work, in addition to their regular classes, but they were keen and the lessons were superb and they liked to see Galvinston grin as he explained some new concept at the blackboard. They also felt special, singled out. Like the Renaissance masters, Galvinston felt responsible for the entire education of his apprentices, so he kept in the basement a bookcase of novels, which they would read and discuss when they were stumped on the physics problems.

Bill had a curious mental condition. In ninth grade, he had slipped in the bathroom, banged his head on the tile floor, and stayed in a coma for ten days. When he gained consciousness, his mind was in good order except that he couldn't recognize people out of their usual context.

Bill knew Bennett from the lab, and when he met him in the lab he recognized him immediately. But when he met Bennett walking across campus or in the dining hall or even in Galvinston's basement, Bennett would have to introduce himself every time. He'd say,

Hi, Bill, and Bill would stop, look bewildered, and ask, Could you tell me where I know you from? Then Bennett would say, Bennett from the lab, and Bill would say, Oh, yes, Bennett, and remember everything. But if Bennett didn't attach the lab to his name, Bill couldn't find the memory. Eventually, whenever Bennett chanced to meet his lab partner outside the lab, he'd say right away, I'm Bennett from the lab.

Each acquaintance of Bill's had his own place label. Stuart was identifiable in the dorm suite, but nowhere else. Professor Michels, Bill's thermodynamics teacher, could be identified anywhere in Jefferson Hall, the physics building. Professor Davidson, his history teacher, was recognizable only in the laundromat on Lincoln Street, where Bill had first met him. Professor Kurfess could be identified in the central reading room of the library.

Bill first met Bennett in freshman physics lab. After that, he recognized Bennett in any laboratory. Somehow, in the workings of Bill's subconscious mind, the oscilloscopes and springs of physics lab could become the test tubes and centrifuges of chemistry lab. Bennett was Bennett from a lab, any lab.

Bennett sometimes wondered what was the minimum amount of laboratory ambiance needed for Bill to recognize him. Would Bill recognize him in a room with a single Bunsen burner and a lab technician in a white coat? In a room with five Bunsen burners but with people giving monologues from *King Lear*? Bennett had discovered, by experiment, that a single piece of laboratory equipment was not sufficient. He once took a voltmeter with him when he went over to Bill's dormitory room. When he walked in, he didn't say, I'm Bennett from the lab. He simply said, I'm Bennett, and exhibited his voltmeter. It didn't work. Bill got that puzzled look on his face and asked, Could you tell me where I know you from?

Bennett became disgruntled with his label. Why did he have to be Bennett from the lab? He was no good in the lab. His experiments caught fire. He wanted a change in his label. Why couldn't he be Bennett from thermodynamics class, where he was triumphing? Or Bennett from Holster courtyard, a lovely spot where he often sat next to a white dogwood and quietly read. He coaxed Bill into going with him to the courtyard, and he posed there next to the dogwood tree with Bill looking on. See, Bennett said, I'm in Holster courtyard. I'm Bennett from Holster courtyard. A week later, when he encountered his friend in Holster courtyard, Bill didn't recognize him until he said he was Bennett from the lab.

Bill's marijuana use became heavier. In their last

year of college, he was high every time Bennett saw him. He'd traded in the dormitory suite of his junior year for a single, and he rarely left his room. There were always several friends with him. Bennett, no longer Bill's lab partner, visited him a couple of times a week. Bill's room was a dark, demented forest. The lights were off, day and night, except for a rotating blue light in the middle of the room. Bill had taped blankets over the windows to keep out the sun. The air was always thick with smoke, and the blue revolving light would flash through the smoke once a second, like a searchlight through fog. Jimi Hendrix sang from the closet. Bennett would enter the room, stand at the door looking into the smoky darkness, and say, Bennett from the lab. Close the door, Bill would say, you're letting in the light. Bennett would close the door and, as his eyes slowly adapted to the dim light, make out Bill and his entourage lying about on cushions in the corners of the room.

Bennett, my good man, Bill would say, what's happening in the world of science? Not much, his old lab partner would answer. Good, Bill would say, because I wouldn't want to miss anything. A great deal is happening right in this very room, but it's happening very slowly. Yessiree, one of Bill's friends would say. Stay a while, Bennett, Bill said. Take off your shoes. Bennett would take off his shoes, sit down on a cushion.

Tell us about quarks, one of Bill's followers would say solemnly from his cushion in the corner, and Bill would launch into an elaborate treatise on subatomic physics, his audience listening in rapt attention, except for the occasional gasp when someone inhaled on the circulating joint. After one or two Hendrix songs and further explanations of the cosmos, Bennett would say, Bill, you've got to stop smoking dope. You're wasting yourself. At this rude remark, one of Bill's friends would moan something like, Shit, Prudhomme, who is this jerk? and Bill would say, Bennett's my lab partner, he's okay.

Bill, you've got to quit this stuff, Bennett would say again. I can quit anytime I want, said Bill. Okay, Bennett said, quit by next Tuesday. Bill would say, I could quit by next Tuesday if I wanted, but I don't want to. You don't want to because you can't, his old lab partner would reply. All right, I'll quit by next Tuesday, said Bill. For you.

Bennett would come back on Tuesday, would penetrate the thick fog in Bill's room. I thought you were going to quit smoking on Tuesday, he said. I was, said Bill, and I could have. I certainly could have. But I changed my mind. I can quit anytime I want to. You can't, Bennett shouted over Hendrix's guitar. You're wasting your mind. Bill shouted back, I'll quit next Tuesday. You're a stupid jerk, Bennett said. You sure had me fooled. I'll quit by next Tuesday, said Bill. Then Bennett would leave, slamming the door.

This went on for months. Bennett got more and more angry. He said some cruel things, which he later regretted. He hated the ruin of Bill's talent. But even more, he hated Bill's loss of control.

Bennett made his friend a withdrawal schedule, which allowed him to reduce his marijuana habit to zero over a period of a month. The plan turned out to be useless, like Bennett's calculations for his uncle. All that changed from week to week was the ever-increasing height of Bill's mail outside his door, including unopened letters from the dean.

The last time Bennett went to his old lab partner's dormitory room, in early May, he announced himself at the door simply as Bennett. Could you tell me where I know you from? came a voice, floating through the sweet-smelling haze. I'm just Bennett, Bennett said, and left.

**B**ennett was practically living at his desk in Galvinston's basement. Occasionally, he would leave to attend a bothersome class, as if to swat a mosquito, then return to the basement. The real learning was there in that room, with Galvinston's tutorials and Bennett's own reading and the magical calculations he did at his desk. Gradually, he was confirming his suspicion that the world was described by equations. He calculated the Raleigh scattering that explained the blue of the sky, the gravitational torques that explained the precession of the equinoxes, the quantum probability for an alpha particle to penetrate an atomic nucleus.

Sometimes, for amusement, he would compute mundane phenomena such as the trajectory of a paper wad.

His Uncle Malcolm, in Memphis, wrote and asked him for help with determining the most profitable way to set inventories in the store. Too many items left at the end of a season and they would lose on the markdowns, but too little stock and they would lose on the sales. And different manufacturers had different lead times for orders. Malcolm had handled the inventory for years, by trial and error, but he was receiving a great deal of criticism these days and wondered whether his scientific nephew might have any ideas. Bennett read Uncle Malcolm's letter at his desk in the morning and within thirty minutes had written down two calculus equations and solved them and phoned his uncle with the optimum strategy. He had never felt so powerful in his life.

After Bill drifted away, Bennett was often alone in the basement, contentedly at work in the evenings until midnight, on weekends. He kept cans of tuna fish in a drawer. Saturdays or Sundays, Galvinston appeared. You're going all the way, Galvinston would say when he saw Bennett, You've got escape velocity. The assistant professor might stride over to Bennett's desk or pace near the blackboard a few minutes. Then he would go to his own desk, take out a thick pad of white, unlined paper, and begin his own calculations, shaking his leg under the table as he worked. With Galvinston, Bennett didn't have to explain why he preferred his desk in the basement over New York with a girl or Cantrell Gymnasium hollering Rumpah Blaineys. Galvinston understood. As Bennett was learning, every professional physicist under forty ate and drank science. After forty, a theoretical physicist might coast a little to indulge in a hobby or spend time with a family. But until then, there was no slowing down. The obsession was part of the ethic. Galvinston, like Bennett, was obsessed. But for some reason he had not yet produced any major piece of work. He was already thirty.

In the spring of his senior year, Bennett decided to stay on at Blaine for graduate work in physics. Most people advised him against it. He should go someplace new, like the West Coast. But Bennett was not taking advice. He didn't want to go someplace new or to meet anyone new. He wanted to burrow into his solitude and quietly celebrate physics. Besides, Blaine had an excellent graduate program. Bennett stayed. Galvinston left. Galvinston had failed to get promoted. They don't value teaching, he said bitterly on the day he was packing. Galvinston was a fine teacher and dedicated to his students, yet Bennett secretly disdained him for not succeeding in research. The glory of science was research.

When Galvinston left, the administration cleaned out his subterranean room, as if a large rat had been holed up there, and converted it into a computer laboratory. Bennett moved down the hall to another room without windows. His new office was about ten feet by ten feet. It had a desk and a brown couch, left by a previous graduate student. There was a blackboard. For decoration, Bennett bought a large plastic plant with red and green leaves and an indecent poster involving Popeye and Olive Oyl.

Bennett had been given an apprentice research problem by Professor Davis Jacoby, a brilliant theoretical physicist at Blaine. Bennett was to generalize a problem tackled earlier by a British scientist: Suppose that some identical particles are placed inside a spherical container. The particles have energy and fly about. At the same time, they pull on each other gravitationally. Initially, the particles will behave like an angry swarm of bees, bunching up first in one place, then in another. Eventually, however, they settle down and stop bunching and come into balance. The question is: How are the particles located after achieving this balance?

The British scientist had answered the question, through mathematical calculations, and published his results. Along the way, he'd unexpectedly discovered that if the total energy of the particles was less than a critical amount, they would *never* come into balance. In this case, some particles would continue congregating more and more densely at the center of the sphere, ad infinitum, and others would race about the perimeter ever more violently, ad infinitum. This frightening possibility came to be called the gravothermal catastrophe. It was all theoretical. But, then, so were the first calculations of the A-bomb.

Bennett's assignment was to re-solve the problem when the particles were not identical but instead came in a mixture of light particles and heavy ones. Unlike the bug problem, or any of his college assignments, the answer to this problem was not known. He could not look it up in a book. The solution might take months. But if he succeeded, Professor Jacoby would accept him as one of his half-dozen doctoral students.

Professor Jacoby requisitioned Bennett's necessary equipment, which consisted of a large stock of white, unlined paper and a wastebasket, and turned Bennett loose on his own.

This apprentice problem was far more interesting than the bug problem. But what did it apply to?

What did it mean? After sitting at his desk for a few days, Bennett walked up to the ground floor of the physics building and softly knocked on the professor's half-opened door.

Professor Jacoby stood up from his desk and smiled. Davis Jacoby was a thin, wiry man with curly blond hair. He was forty. He wore raucous Hawaiian shirts, left over from his years at UC Berkeley. Everyone knew that Jacoby was itching to get back to California. The rumor was that he'd been tossed out of Berkeley for sleeping with the wife of one of his graduate students. Bennett found this story astonishing because it would have transpired during the very same period when Jacoby accomplished his famous work on space-time singularities.

After listening to Bennett's questions, Jacoby was willing to reveal that the imaginary particles corresponded to a cluster of stars, all orbiting each other under their mutual gravity, each star being represented by one particle in Bennett's problem. Star clusters had been seen through telescopes. It had been estimated that the orbit of an individual star in a cluster might take a hundred thousand years, but that was a drop in the bucket because the universe was ten billion years old. But how could a huge gaseous thing like a star be replaced by a tiny particle in his calculations, asked Bennett. An approximation, said Jacoby. And what about the container? What was that? Bennett wasn't aware that astronomers had spotted any vast, cosmic spheres floating in space, holding millions of stars. Professor Jacoby allowed that the giant container was a fiction, but he argued that it made the problem clean and mathematically tractable. Furthermore, once the gravo-thermal catastrophe got under way, the container wouldn't matter anyway. Yes. And why was Bennett re-doing the problem with a mixture of particles of different weights? Oh, said Jacoby, gesturing expansively with his arms, we want to be as realistic as possible. It's well known that real star clusters have a mixture of stars.

Within a couple of weeks, Bennett was happily lost in a world of conjecture. He could write down an equation on his white pad of paper and ten thousand stars would appear, careening through space. Or he could add a mathematical symbol and the stars would bounce off the walls of a great cosmic vessel. If he paused to eat tuna fish, the stars suddenly froze—ten thousand suns held in suspended animation—until he swallowed his last bite and returned to his calculations.

He soon realized that his problem was not of fundamental importance. And the basic attack had already been mapped by another scientist before. But he was confronting a problem that had never been solved.

There was so much of the world that people took on faith. Bennett understood that he had to trust others for much that he knew. But every unverified fact extracted a small price. Little by little, he had been paying away his independence and self-confidence. Now he had a chance to discover something true about the world, absolutely true, taking nobody's word for it. He soared. He relished his problem with the particles and the sphere, and he carried his pages of calculations around with him everywhere, as if they were heirloom letters.

Several other new physics graduate students were also being sized up by Professor Jacoby, each obsessed with his own apprentice problem. They all had tiny offices in the same area of Jefferson basement, had all finished their first year of courses. There was an Indian, Dalip Chandra, who was miraculously supporting a family back in India on his small student stipend. To save money, he lived in his office. Let us think about this more carefully, he would say in his quiet voice. After a year, his wife got ill and he had to go back to India. There was a young man from New York with thinning hair and black-framed eyeglasses, which he looked over when he spoke. Early in his second year, he announced that his courses had been trivial. When he heard Bennett's problem about the particles and sphere, he said that it also was trivial. There was a fellow from California, thin as a broom, with a blond ponytail. Jenkins. He didn't spend any time in his office. He was always sitting on a bench outdoors under the Jefferson arch, sitting and staring off and apparently doing nothing. But he was thinking. He went on to a remarkable scientific career. A young man named Hamilton from the Midwest was constantly writing pages and pages of equations. He could scribble while walking. He wrote on lined paper, unlike everybody else, and his equations were very close together, very dense and hard to read, like microfilm of military secrets. Hamilton never boasted or bragged, but he had such inner confidence that he did his calculations in pen.

The apprentices didn't socialize. They were struggling to prove themselves, to earn respect from the master, and they had to do it alone. Later, those accepted into Jacoby's group would join a community, would be in and out of each other's offices constantly, discussing their research, new developments in physics, the latest journal articles and preprints. But at this time they hadn't solved any real problems, they hadn't shown they could make it in science, and they were not part of the group. They worked by themselves, each in his own tiny office, and their obsessions were private.

## Good Benito

Bennett lived in a studio apartment not far past the edge of the campus. He spent little time there. He slept there. He showered there, got dressed in the morning, received letters from his mother and occasionally his brothers. The refrigerator remained empty, except for some cans of Coca-Cola and a box of baking soda.

Bennett liked walking home late at night. He followed a stone path that wound through campus, past fountains, through courtyards, past the library, the old stone cathedral. The path was lit by gas lamps on both sides. On fall evenings, a fine mist often hovered in the air, and the mist glowed pink from the gas lanterns. In winter, great mounds of snow rose high on both sides of the path, forming a white tunnel. He sometimes imagined that he was walking through underground tunnels on the moon. Beyond campus, he followed Bow Street until it met Silver Lane and his apartment. It was a lovely walk and the only few moments of the day when he stopped thinking of physics. He sometimes thought about Leila and whether she missed him, and John. The town went to bed early, leaving the stretch along Bow Street quite dark. On clear nights, he would sit on the front steps when he got home and breathe in the night air and look up at the sharp, silent stars, magnificent and uncontained.

**M**any days, Bennett's only outing from his small office in Jefferson basement was to walk down the hall to pick up his telephone messages. His office did not have a telephone. The previous occupant of the room, a bearded and exceedingly quiet young man from South Africa, had rewired the telephone jack for some unexplained purpose and rendered it totally useless for ordinary communications. Bennett's telephone had been relocated in another office down the hall.

His messages would read something like: Professor Thules says that the space-time singularity is actually two-dimensional, which can be seen from an inordinate transformation. Are you sure you've got his name right? Bennett would ask Jellison, who worked in the office and had written down the message. Could it have been Leonard Thalp from Minnesota? Jellison would crane his neck around momentarily and then go back to his accounts. Jellison had worked contract accounts for the physics department for twenty-five years and had seen many generations of graduate students come and go. You've got inordinate transformation written here, continued Bennett, should it have been coordinate transformation? I'm not your secretary, said Jellison without looking up. I've got calls coming on my own line.

Bennett did not mind dealing with Jellison, nor did he mind walking down the hall to get his messages, but he hated the imprecision of the messages. Jellison always got something wrong. Bennett wanted complete accuracy. He wanted his messages exactly right. So he got a telephone answering machine. He set it at zero rings.

He began waiting until late at night, when he was on his way home, to play back his messages for the day. He would unlock Jellison's dark office, sit in the small pine chair near the door, and listen to the recordings in the half-light that seeped in from the hall.

One evening, quite late, when the building was

silent and empty, Bennett pushed the play button of his machine and got the following message: Thank you, I got the books. [Long pause] I've been debating about whether to call you. I want to apologize for the way I acted. [Pause] I'm kind of ashamed. I don't know why I act like that. I don't want you to think I'm a bad person. I'm not really a bad person. [Long pause] I just don't behave right with other people sometimes. I don't know why I act the way I do. I'm not a bad person. [Pause] Goodbye. You don't have to respond.

No name was given. It was the voice of a man with a slight foreign accent. Bennett didn't recognize the voice. He sat in the dim light and played back the tape several times, puzzled. Finally, he erased it and went home. But the message haunted him. That voice ached. Whose was it? What did the message mean? Had he sent books to someone, perhaps months ago, and forgotten? Surely it was left by mistake, was not intended for him. But he couldn't get it out of his mind. Did he know this man? Did he know this man?

Three months into his project, Bennett hit a snag. He'd set up all the equations and begun solving them, but something was wrong. He knew that if he made his two groups of particles identical to each other, then his problem reduced to the same one the British scientist had solved, and, indeed, his equations were the same. But when he solved those equations, he didn't get the same answer. Therefore, an error had to be lurking somewhere. He checked his calculations but couldn't find a mistake. But there had to be a mistake.

Next morning, he walked to his office earlier than usual and left his briefcase by the door and sharpened his pencils a long time while he thought through the problem once more. He sipped coffee from a Styrofoam cup. Then he sat at his desk and checked his equations again. He worked through the morning and had a pizza delivered and kept working. People were talking down the hall, undergraduates, and he closed his door and then opened it again because the room became hot. He couldn't find a mistake. He went out briefly for dinner and saw no one he knew. That evening, he brooded as he walked home along the pretty winding path past the fountains, the courtyards, the library, the old stone cathedral. He felt foolish and angry at himself. This was a straightforward problem. Jacoby had told him so.

When he arrived at his office the next morning, he sharpened his pencils again and put down his cup of coffee and slammed his fist on the desk. There's a mistake in here, he said to the blackboard. I know there's a mistake in here, and today is the day I'm going to find it. He ripped a leaf off the red plastic plant and rammed its plastic stem through his Styrofoam cup, spilling the black coffee on his desk. Then he cleaned up the coffee and the bits of Styrofoam and got to work, starting back at the first equation and going forward. He tortured each equation, one by one, until it told him it was true. Then he went to the next. Often, he'd rederive some equations from scratch, on separate sheets of white, unlined paper. After checking a page, he wadded it up, very tight, and threw it in the direction of the wastebasket. He went through a lot of paper. Late that evening, having failed to find any error, he again pounded his fist on the desk and pushed the papers into his briefcase and walked home. He couldn't sleep. He slept a half-sleep, with dreams of sitting at his desk and then a waking awareness of his body in bed and his failure and his fear of never finding his mistake and leaving Blaine in disgrace.

In the morning, he studied the British scientist's paper over and over, asked himself what he could possibly be doing wrong. He sharpened his pencils and opened his briefcase and started again. The noise outside, people talking, bothered him again and he decided to keep his door closed and just live with the heat.

This went on for two months. Eventually, he memorized the equations.

Occasionally, he had the urge to ask for help, to discuss his predicament with one of the other students or with Professor Jacoby. But he couldn't. This was a straightforward calculation. He couldn't ask for help on an elementary problem. Once, he even got as far as Jacoby's door, his crumpled calculations in hand. But he couldn't go further. When he passed his fellow apprentices, he looked down at the floor. Surely they were making more progress on their problems. He had the sickening feeling that he didn't have what it took.

Unaccountably, he began spending a great deal of time away from his office, at a public park two miles from campus. The park had a Japanese garden. He would sit near a little red bridge, crossing a stream, and listen to the tinkling of the water over rocks. He would study the ground where he sat, admire a ladybug as it crawled along a thin blade of grass. The water was music. He imagined that its tone slightly changed with minute variations in the stream, tiny bits of debris, puffs of wind. He imagined he was hearing a symphony. While the water symphony played, he would look at the passing mothers with their strollers. They seemed happy in their lives. They would linger to look at the nasturtiums or to drop small stones in the stream. The mothers would stop leisurely to secure the caps on their babies, exchange pleasant conversation, laugh, and walk on. The air smelled like fresh lemon. He wanted to stay. Day after day, he kept coming back to the park, to see the happiness of the mothers and to smell the fresh lemon smell and to listen to the tinkling of the water.

**H**e was taking a shower in his apartment before breakfast. Suddenly his body turned light as a feather. His head lifted up off his shoulders, and he felt like the time he had planed in a sailboat. The boat had been traveling at normal speed, but the wind was extremely high. Without warning the hull lifted out of the water and the drag instantly dropped to near zero and the boat began flying, as if some giant hand had grabbed hold of the mast and flung the boat over the surface like a skimming stone.

He was planing. He sank down on the tiles, with the water pouring over his head, and saw his error as well as the entire solution to his problem. A mixture of particles was more fragile than a pure population; a mixture made the gravothermal catastrophe more likely to happen. The answer appeared in his mind as a beautiful curve and he tingled and shivered. It had to be right. He leaped out of the shower. Without bothering to get dressed, or even to dry off, he went to the kitchen table and got out his pages of calculations and a new pad of white paper and began writing. He lost track of time, he lost track of his body. He was completely outside of himself, outside of the world. Within two hours he had reworked his problem in complete quantitative detail. Shaking, he graphed the solution and it matched the arc in his mind. The equations, which over the last months had grown tired and suspicious, came to life, and they were right and they were graceful and they glistened like a moon over trees.

He never understood how he had found his mistake, but it wasn't by going from one equation to the next. Somehow, his subconscious mind had been studying the problem in its own slender way, spotted an error, and then danced to the answer. A year later, he decided that the problem was indeed trivial, as the fellow student had said. And the sacrament of certainty was perhaps just an illusion. But the sensation of planing, that swift soaring breath of discovery, was not an illusion. It was real. And for a while he, the discoverer, was the only person on earth who knew this new thing. He would soon get dressed and go to his office, he would soon take his results to Professor Jacoby and tell his colleagues, he would soon publish his results in the *Physical Review*. But for those first few moments at his kitchen table, he was alone with his discovery, he knew something true that no one else knew, and he had vast power in the world.

**D**avis Jacoby was magnetic. When he looked at you, you had a compelling sense that something big was about to happen, you wanted to stay near him. This quality, as much as his achievements in physics, attracted students to him from all over the world. Now just a little past forty, he had already trained several generations of top young physicists and was one of those few scientists who had fostered a school. Schools of methodology were rare in science, where the ultimate goal was the disembodied equation, the reproducible experiment. Conventional wisdom held that personal style was irrelevant. Likewise pedigrees and lineages of students and teachers. Jacoby, on the other hand, considered mentorship extremely important. He always reminded his new students that he had been a student of Leonid Baliv, after his escape to the U.S., and that Baliv had studied with the great Russian theorist Lev Davidovich Landau.

Davis's philosophy of mentoring was mainly to let his students teach themselves. Create a critical mass of brilliant graduate students. Then duck for cover. His only requirement, which he never stated out loud, was that the office doors of his students had to stay open. That way, the chain reactions could fly unimpeded.

Davis kept his own door open as well. When Bennett finished his apprentice problem with the particles and the sphere, he walked in. Davis was sitting at his desk, wearing his shirt with the blue and green toucans. He peered over a tall stack of paper, the giant textbook he'd been laboring over for a decade. Everytime the book was near completion, he'd get wind of a new development, at the cutting edge, and insist on including it. The colossus was now projected to run over twelve hundred pages, well past the point where it could be priced affordably for students.

The professor greeted Bennett warmly. Looks like you've got something to show me, he said happily, and carefully moved aside the mountain of manuscript on his desk. He began perusing Bennett's graphs and equations, saying, Yes, I see. I see. Then, after five minutes, he looked up and said, Very nice. You should write this up and submit it to the *Physical Review.* Dolores will type it. Then he reached into a file cabinet and handed Bennett a black notebook. Take it home, he said, and pick out your next problem.

Bennett had heard about the black book. It was shown only to students who worked directly with Davis. The black notebook held the celebrated Jacoby Conundrums, a collection of important, unsolved problems in theoretical physics. Significant research problems were often no more difficult to solve than insignificant ones. You just needed a nose for the right questions. A doctoral thesis problem chosen from the black notebook had guaranteed significance.

Bennett was floating. He made a mental note that he must immediately write to John and tell him about this moment. Is your office comfortable? said Davis. Fine, said Bennett. We've got some young hotshots around here, said Davis, grinning. You just solved a difficult problem. He shook Bennett's hand. Bennett mumbled something about how proud he was to be working with Davis and tucked the black notebook under his arm and went outside. He walked a long time in the yellow sunlight and then sat under a tree and began his letter to John, which John of course would not answer. Then, irresistably, he put down his pencil and began paging through the Jacoby Conundrums.


Davis's own research he usually did away from the office. However, there was no doubt about which problems he was keen on. Outside his door, on the walls of the hallway, were various framed wagers between himself and other distinguished physicists: Davis Jacoby wagers Demetrius Sourkis that white holes do not conserve angular momentum; D.J. will forfeit five bottles of Kentucky bourbon and D.S. will forfeit four bottles of Kalvos ouzo. A white hole was about as exotic and hypothetical an object as physicists had dreamed of. But it was typical of what Davis set his mind to. None of his research problems had the slightest practical application. With his abilities in physics and mathematics, he could have named his salary at Los Alamos or Bell Labs or Hewlett Packard. But he refused to work on anything that had possible material consequences within the next hundred years. He liked his physics pure. The research problems in the black notebook were as pure as the ponderings of a Buddhist monk.

Over the years, Davis gradually won all the wagers on the wall. In addition to his technical ability, he possessed a remarkable physical intuition, like a sense of smell. He had a deep physical feeling for the world. He could reduce the most complex phenomenon to a series of spinning tops or springs or water waves, which he visualized in his mind, and he could see straight through a problem. When he suggested a new problem to a student, he would say, I think it's going to come out like this, and he'd outline the solution. He wouldn't give the details. He didn't know the details. But he would box in the answer. Six months or a year later, when the student got the details, they would fit smack into Davis's box. Davis delighted in making such forecasts and seeing them confirmed. On the rare occasions that he was wrong about something, he would stare at the final computer printouts or mathematical solutions with an agitated look on his face, holding his head extremely still. After a while, he would leap up from his desk and slap his forehead and shout gleefully, Of course, what a fool I was! and begin pacing around deep in thought, rearranging the landmarks of his cosmos to accommodate this new bit of knowledge. It seemed to Bennett that Davis took more pleasure in being wrong than right. When he was wrong, he learned something new.

When Bennett returned with the black book,

Davis was hopping around his office with amusement. The Xerox machine was broken. For the last twenty-four hours, all of his students had been sour and broody. It's wonderful, he said, now they'll have to read the journal articles instead of Xeroxing them. Then he waved Bennett to the couch in his office and came over to join him. He walked with a slight limp. The story was that he'd been stricken with some muscular disease when he was eight. He'd had daily physical therapy, using a contraption of pulleys, weights, and gears, and he'd stared at that contraption for hours on end. Then he improved it. Then he became a physicist.

I want to do the problem on gravitational radiation in strong fields, said Bennett. Good, said Davis, what are your boundary conditions at infinity? Bennett looked perplexed. He knew about boundary conditions from undergraduate physics, but he wasn't aware that this problem needed any. The problem isn't well posed, said Davis, unless you specify the fields at infinity. You've got to specify a problem in enough detail so that it clearly has a definite solution. That's a well-posed problem. That's what you want. Your problem with the particles and the sphere, for example, wouldn't have been well posed without knowing the total energy of the particles. Davis paused, as if remembering something. Some questions, he said, can never be well posed, like: Is there a God? or, Would we be happier if we lived longer?

Just then, the secretary walked in. Jenny's on the phone, the secretary said. She's been unable to get through on 7836, and it's urgent. Tell her I'll call back in half an hour, Davis said. Jenny was his mother. He continued his tutorial. You want to know that your problem has a definite answer before you begin work on it. Never waste time on a poorly posed problem.

Bennett nodded. When he returned to his office, he sat down on the floor and thought about what his professor had said and decided that he had never met anyone as wise as Davis Jacoby. He would learn all he could from the master. First off, he made an oath to himself that never again would he fritter away one minute on a poorly posed problem.


Davis lived in a great house on Taylor Street. He lived alone. Occasionally, a woman would briefly move in with him, but no relationship lasted more than six months. All of his students knew his big house on Taylor, for that was the setting of his parties. The house was extraordinary, bought with money he had inherited from a rich uncle. It was a modern-style mansion, completely misplaced in its neighborhood. The outside was white stucco, with a broad front veranda under angled circular windows. The inside had countless rooms and split-level balconies perched at surprising locations and a Jacuzzi in the center of the house. Large blue and green enamel vases with ferns occupied the hallways.

At Davis's parties, a young graduate student could meet the best physicists in the world, often drunk. There Bennett met Demetrius Sourkis, after he'd lost his bet. Sourkis had known Einstein personally, and he held a dozen students enraptured for an hour with stories of Einstein's latter years at the Institute for Advanced Study. After telling his stories, Professor Sourkis went to sleep on a couch. At Davis's house, Bennett once met Igor Stroblich, on his way to attend a conference at the University of Chicago. Stroblich had discovered the Stroblich gauge for axion fields and could solve differential equations in his head. He installed himself in an empty room upstairs, and Davis's students filed in to see him, one by one, each spending twenty minutes with him discussing their research. Three hours later, Stroblich emerged and had a tall glass of bourbon and announced loudly that he admired the U.S. and that the U.S. and Russia could save money if they combined spy satellites.

•   •   •

In Bennett's last year, Davis finally finished his monu-
mental textbook and suddenly began acting strangely.
When an invitation came for him to give a major address at the annual meeting of the American Physical
Society, he startled Bennett and some other of his students by yelling at Dolores to refuse the invitation.
Who's got time to prepare a talk for Miami? he shouted
from the door of his office. Don't they think I'm doing
research anymore? A week later, he was asked to serve
on a committee of the National Academy of Sciences.
He got so angry he didn't even return the call.

He began working harder and harder at his own
research, driving himself at the frantic pace of his students. He began staying at school every night, in his own
office, closing his door. One night at midnight, Bennett
was coming out of the reference room when he saw
Davis emerge from his office with bloodshot eyes and a
bitter look on his face. Bennett hardly recognized him.
Davis said hello, an odd look of embarrassment swept
over his face, and he hurried down the hall. A week later,
Tarker, a third-year student, showed up with an elegant
solution to the same problem Davis had been working
on himself. Davis congratulated Tarker profusely. But
he didn't come out of his office until the next morning.
He began putting his name last on joint papers with his
students, or crossing his name off altogether.

Eventually, Davis stopped publishing altogether, but he remained at Blaine many more years. And his framed wagers remained on the wall, one or two being retired every year as he gradually saw proved the insightful conjectures he'd made in his youth.

When Bennett finished his doctoral thesis, Davis of course gave him a party. A lot of people came. Bennett had made sure of that, by sending invitations to acquaintances of acquaintances, people he didn't know at all.

It was a very warm night in June. The windows were open. Every once in a while, a neighbor would knock at the door and demand that the music be turned down. Davis would invite the neighbor in and offer him beer. We've got a new doctor of philosophy tonight, he said loudly and called for Bennett. Someone hollered, Need a quantum mechanic? What, we're out of beer? discovered Davis. How can that be? He dispatched a graduate student to Limo's to get more beer and pizza.

People took off their shoes and danced. A professor had brought Steely Dan and Fleetwood Mac albums. Some people sat in chairs talking physics or waiting for the next car from Limo's to come with more beer. Two couples no one knew went directly to the Jacuzzi room as soon as they arrived, stripped down to their underwear, and sat in the hot water drinking champagne.

Bennett had been crowned by a western cowboy hat with a diploma dangling from it. He was elated. He walked from room to room, greeting everyone and accepting congratulations. He was full of beer. He went to the bathroom and suddenly wished that John were there and sat on the toilet, composing a letter to John. I've just got my degree, his letter began. I'm at this wonderful party. I don't have any friends at the party. Why don't you write me, you asshole. Bennett got up and went back to the party.

It was getting hot with the dancing and the noise. Flies buzzed through the open windows, drawn by the pizza and spilled beer. In the living room, a belly dancer gyrated to a Rolling Stones album. What, we're out of beer again? shouted Davis from somewhere in the house. A postdoctoral fellow was sent to Limo's to pick up more beer.

A photographer acquaintance of Davis's arrived, carrying several cameras around his neck. Someone explained that he was an intellectual, a man who read widely and considered it an obligation to photograph members of the academic establishment. Some of his photographs had been collected in a book. The photographer set up his tripod. Immediately flies descended on his equipment, which smelled strangely. What's happening here? he shouted, trying to shoo away the insects without knocking down his tripod. One of the women who'd been lounging in the Jacuzzi tiptoed in and draped a damp towel over the photographer's camera. What's happening here? he shouted again. Then, turning to no one in particular, he said, If I had money, I'd be a great man. Here's a beer, Steven, said Davis happily, why don't you dance with someone?

A little after midnight, the physicist Andrzej Baleski committed the error of challenging Davis to a drinking bout. Straight vodka. Baleski had been teaching a graduate course in quantum physics at Blaine for the semester and was about to return to Warsaw. Baleski could drink. Davis, however, had visited Stroblich in Moscow and had learned how to really drink. After the first bottle, it was clear that Davis had won, but he wouldn't let Baleski bow out. He was ruthless. He played on Baleski's pride, well into the second bottle. Finally, Baleski began throwing up on the orange Navajo carpet and stumbled away, without admitting defeat.

Even with close to a quart of vodka in his veins, Davis was in fine form. Tonight, he felt young and capable of anything. We need more beer, he bellowed, without looking in the kitchen, and sent another student to Limo's. He patted Bennett on the back, again toasted his thesis, and led him to one of the sitting rooms, where a cosmological discussion was in progress. A graduate student named Price had seized upon the informality of the setting to ask the professors some embarrassing questions. When Davis walked in, Price immediately steered him into a corner. How would you design the universe if you could do it any way you wanted? asked Price. Price had an unusual poetic bent. That's a hell of a question, roared Davis. But he was intrigued. He sat down in a red leather chair and began thinking. A dozen students and professors gathered around him, belching, and waited for his answer.

Finally, Davis said, I'd make the universe much larger. It's too small. Too small? asked Price. We understand space pretty well out to two million light years, said Davis. The Andromeda galaxy lies at that distance. It's the nearest big galaxy, we have excellent photos of it, we know what it's made of. Well, the size of the entire observable universe is only five thousand times further out than Andromeda. That's not a big number. It could have been five trillion times further. Or five zillion. I find the universe confining. I'd have made it much bigger. The universe is too small.

With Davis's last sentence, Bennett smelled the

vodka, and he was suddenly somewhere else. He was a child, in his bed, and Florida was gingerly stroking his head with a towel soaked in alcohol, stroking and singing her sad, beautiful song.

**B**ennett took out the cigar box beside his bed. The Scalapino affair was a year in the past, and he had recently moved to a house in southwest Baltimore. He gingerly held the box and studied the old, familiar pictures. His father on the front porch. His father and mother walking on the beach. His father in the naval uniform. He remembered the story Sidney had told him years ago, when he was twelve or thirteen. The two of them had been home alone at the kitchen table, eating their lunch, when Sidney unexpectedly began telling Bennett about a terrible incident in World War II. Sidney never said more than a few sentences to Bennett, before then or since, but on that day in the kitchen he told his son a story in such graphic detail that Bennett could always recall it exactly.

It was September 9, 1943, the invasion of Salerno. Sidney was an ensign in the navy. He was stationed on the ship *Orion* and commanded a number of landing craft. These craft were about fifty feet long, blue-gray, and carried men and supplies from the transport ships to the beach under barrage. During a landing, the transport ships would approach the enemy beach to within about ten miles, just beyond range of artillery, then anchor and dispatch their invading forces to shore aboard the landing craft. The landing craft were good targets. Artillery shelled them. Enemy aircraft flew over and strafed them. It was easier and more efficient to kill men huddled together in a small boat than spread out on the beach after they'd landed. For defense, each craft had two .50-caliber machine guns mounted behind armor-plated shields, but the men had only seconds to spot attacking planes, and the artillery shells came out of nowhere. Invisible death could also strike from the submerged mines near the shore.

Each wave of landing craft traveled together, and their movements needed to be coordinated. That was Sidney's job. He rode in one boat and gave navigational orders to the others, using hand signals. After his boats reached the shore and emptied themselves, he would travel back to the *Orion* or a nearby transport ship and load up with more men and supplies.

On September 9, 1943, the United States Fifth Army, borne by the *Orion* and five hundred other U.S. warships, attacked the coastal city of Salerno, in an attempt to drive the Germans north, out of Italy. Sidney's orders were to pick up troops from the transport ship *Edgar Allan Poe,* land them at a certain position on the coast called Green Beach Two, then return to the *Orion.* Green Beach Two would be hot, but it was vital that Sidney's troops land at that precise location to build a key section of road for advancing American troops.

Sidney picked up his requisite troops. As he was circling the transport for the last time before heading out, the captain of the *Edgar Allan Poe* got on the P.A. and ordered all boats in the vicinity to return to his ship after dropping their first loads.

Then the invasion began. Sidney gathered his boats and gave instructions to weave back and forth toward the shore. Warplanes could be heard in the distance. Salerno Bay had a terrible beauty, its curving shoreline rising abruptly from the sea, its sands dead white. About two miles in, a U.S. patrol boat whooshed by and created a protective smoke screen for the incoming boats.

When they emerged on the other side of the

smoke, about a half mile from shore, pandemonium. Just ahead, a large landing craft half on the beach was being ripped apart by artillery shells. The boat was on fire, and bodies floated around it. On a bluff above the beach sat a string of German tanks with 88-millimeter cannons. Sidney could see them through his binoculars. Every few seconds, one of the tanks flashed, making a tiny light in the distance. Then a shell whistled through the air and exploded. Suddenly a shell crashed into the ocean just ten yards in front of Sidney's boat. Water sprayed in. The boat rocked violently, the air sagged with the pungency of cordite. Ten seconds later, another shell crashed close behind. More spray. Their position had been bracketed. The German tanks were good at their work.

In the next five seconds, Sidney decided to order his boats to fall back out of range of the 88s. His throat was so dry that he could hardly talk. He mumbled the words to the signal man. The boats turned around. Most of his men were so frightened that their eyes were glazed over, but the coxswain shot him an intense look, enigmatic. Was it a questioning look? Or a look of disgust? The boats retreated, as commanded. Eventually, they landed at a less hostile beach two miles up the coast and returned to the *Edgar Allan Poe* for a second load.

Two days later, Sidney was called to the captain's quarters on the *Orion*. When he walked in, the captain was sitting behind his circular desk. The captain was a man in his fifties, heavily built and handsome with white hair. He had the confident air of Sidney's father, who often bragged that his son was an officer in the navy.

The captain of the *Orion* sat at his desk with his hands clasped, looked straight at the young ensign when he walked in. Please close the door, mister, said the captain. The captain leaned over to tie his shoe, then looked again at Sidney. Mister, your actions day before yesterday may have cost us lives. Sidney began trembling. The captain continued, Why didn't you come back to the *Orion* according to orders?

I got orders from the captain of the *Edgar Allan Poe* to return to his ship for another load, said Bennett's father. The older man pounded his desk. The captain of the *Edgar Allan Poe* had no right! he shouted. That man is an idiot. This is where you should have come. Do you understand? Yes, Captain, said Sidney. That is all, mister, said the captain.

Outside the captain's door, Sidney leaned against the bulkhead and nearly collapsed. He hadn't slept for two days. Miraculously, the captain had not mentioned his retreat. The captain had not mentioned his retreat. But he didn't need to.

## Good Benito

In Sidney's remaining time in the navy, one or another of the men whom he'd commanded at Salerno would occasionally come up to him and say, I would have done the same as you, I wouldn't have landed on that beach. Sidney wouldn't talk about it. And he never talked about it, until that afternoon with his son.

Sidney hadn't looked at Bennett as he told the story. He looked down at his plate. Afterwards, the two of them sat without talking. Then Sidney abruptly said that he'd never lived up to his father's expectations. Then he said that he wished he had died in his boat in the invasion of Salerno.

Bennett's stomach turned into an anvil inside of him. He wanted to scrape away part of his body. He wanted to say something. He wanted to put his arms around his father. But he could only sit there in silence.

**B**ennett heard a loud whirring sound. He was irritated with the intrusion when he was trying to think. And now, at eleven in the evening, even with the blinds down and his office door closed, his ears would not leave his mind alone. He covered an ear with one hand and scribbled equations with the other. But that still left one ear exposed to the loud whirring sound.

Following the sound, he got up from his desk and went across the hall, to the tape room. Garfund was there, doing something to one of his tapes. Exercising the tapes, shouted Garfund, not waiting for Bennett to ask. Now, please leave me alone. Or help.

Garfund was sweating heavily and had unbuttoned his shirt. The computer tapes, which were normally stored in the gray metal shelves, were stacked up on tables. Hundreds of them. Garfund was running a tape reel to reel through a vacuum drive, which whined and whirred.

Three years of data, he said, with a grim look on his face. I can't lose it. He took out a handkerchief and wiped the sweat off his hands, then off his bald head.

What happened? asked Bennett. Here, shouted Garfund. Hold this and wind here when I tell you. What happened? asked Bennett again. The tapes are disintegrating, said Garfund. Last night I started a data reduction using one of the tapes. I got garbage. It was totally gone. I don't know how many others are lost. I've got to exercise them. They can't sit.

I thought the tapes were stored in metal containers, said Bennett. Aren't they protected? The oxide is flaking, said Garfund. Somehow, it got too hot. Or too humid. Maybe precipitation, or dust. Something might be wrong with the humidity control in here. I can't lose this stuff. Three years of data from Astro X.

Astro X was a satellite that had been launched seven years earlier to monitor X-rays from quasars. Its enormous quantities of data had been ultimately inscribed on magnetic tapes, which were divided between

Goddard, Caltech, the University of Chicago, and Leominster. A small, sleepy college like Leominster and a mediocre astrophysicist such as Roland Garfund would never have been entrusted with raw data of that importance, but Garfund had once worked at Goddard and had some connections. Two hundred master tapes had been sent to him. At this point, the satellite had been dead for four years, orbiting aimlessly in space, but its precious data were preserved on celluloid tape and would be studied for the next dozen years. Scientists around the world were anxiously awaiting the analyses of the tapes. Almost weekly, Garfund got calls from the theorists at Princeton and Cambridge.

Bennett had often visited the tape room during his three years at Leominster. Half of the room was filled with tall rows of shelves, holding the tapes. He would walk slowly between the rows, staring at tape after tape, trying to fathom the magnitude of information stored on them, the trillions upon trillions of pieces of information. Some quasars, two thirds the way across the visible universe, had never been identified until Astro X. Their giant plumes of gas, their leviathan energy creation, their entire existence was recorded only in the delicate magnetic blips on those tapes. And since quasars were the most distant objects known in the universe, it might rightly be said that most of the universe lay quietly waiting within the gray metal shelves in Garfund's tape room.

Bennett would walk slowly down the aisles between shelves, gazing long at the tapes, placing his hands on each metal container and trying to imagine the truths it contained, the certainties distilled into numbers. Then, when he became overwhelmed, he would wander into the other half of the room. There, Garfund's astronomy students sat at computer terminals and manipulated images on their screens, digitized pictures of quasars extracted from the tiny fraction of data so far analyzed. The students spoke in hushed tones, as if they were visiting a temple. But their legs twitched excitedly underneath the tables. When a new picture appeared on someone's screen, they would jump up from their chairs to look. Cooo-oool, look at that hot spot, that sucker must be a hundred million degrees. The students were just undergraduates, twenty years old, and here were these quasars, some never before seen by human eyes, billions of light years away, trapped on the computer screens. Many students came to the tape room in midafternoon, bringing canteens of soft drinks and slices of pizza for dinner, arguing about who would get first crack at the new quasar. Yo, look at that X-ray jet. Let's get its coordinates.

Now, except for Garfund and Bennett, the tape

room was empty. The air had a gauzy, blue-green tint from the glow of the terminals. A tape had just finished being run through the vacuum to remove any dust. It was labeled 5C 678, the name of a quasar. Let's see what we've got, said Garfund nervously. He wiped the sweat off his hands again and mounted the tape on another tape drive. They waited. Good, Garfund said softly, This part is good. Good. Good. The tape spun around, its contents flickering in machine language on a digital display. Suddenly, a light flashed, indicating a parity error. Shit, Garfund moaned. Shit, shit, shit. It's still got garbage. I'm in deep shit. Garfund slumped down in a chair, took off his glasses, and stared blankly at the wall.

Bennett picked up some of the hard copy produced by the tape. Each page was covered with numbers. Somewhere in those numbers, now hopelessly lost, was the precise position of 5C 678, the intensity of its X-rays in different locations, in different frequency channels.

Garfund was silent. Bennett didn't know Garfund very well, but he went over and patted his shoulder. Garfund just stared at the wall. Bennett didn't want to leave him like that. He began walking around the room. Garfund lit a cigarette. He had never smoked before in the tape room. No one had.

What's Simdat? Bennett asked, lofting a tape on

the other side of a long table. Simulated data, said Garfund listlessly. Then, after a pause, To see if the systems are working. What does it look like? asked Bennett. Garfund didn't answer, sat smoking and staring at the wall. What does it look like? Bennett repeated. Garfund sighed. It looks like the real thing, he said. The computer creates a fictitious quasar, imitates its detection by Astro X, digitizes the data, puts it on a tape. We then analyze the tape and see if we get the fake quasar back. It's a test.

Could you simulate 5C 678? asked Bennett. I don't really feel like talking, said Garfund. He inhaled deeply on his cigarette and exhaled a huge cloud of smoke. Could you simulate a quasar and call it 5C 678? asked Bennett. Of course I could, said Garfund, turning around to glare at Bennett. But it wouldn't be 5C 678, now would it?

Bennett sat down in a chair at one of the terminals, his face bathed in the blue-green glow of the screen. The quasar project at Leominster was finished. It would be terminated immediately. He found himself imagining the stricken looks of the students. He knew some of them well. They were in his classes.

Let's simulate a whole bunch of quasars, Bennett said quietly. Put them on tape. Don't label them Simdat. Label them from the 5C catalogue. Garfund turned around and stared at Bennett incredulously. Are you crazy? he said. The students wouldn't know, said Bennett. The students, Garfund screamed. The students. What about the National Aeronautics and Space Administration? What about Pinsky at Goddard? What about Thornton at Princeton? Do you think we're playing games? Get out of here. And if you're very good to me, I might not mention what you said.

I was just thinking about the students, Bennett said. Get out of here, shouted Garfund.

**B**ennett peered from his kitchen window, watching the taxicab pull up. Uncle Maury got out. He wore his Dodgers cap and looked much bulkier than Bennett had last seen him. Maury squinted at the number on the mailbox, fumbled in his pocket, and brought out several slips of paper before finding a few crumpled bills for the driver. Then he began walking, slowly dragging his suitcase across the concrete. His suitcase bulged in odd places, no doubt filled with tools.

Bennett hadn't seen his uncle for three years. Last week a letter had come, addressed in the familiar back-slanted handwriting, asking if Maury might visit.

Bennett didn't like visitors. He had a neat, quiet house. He had a routine. He had the purity of his work. But he couldn't say no to Maury. Now he stared out the window as his uncle painstakingly made his way over the curb, along the sidewalk, up the stairs to the walkway. He was thinking that he should go out and help his uncle. Maury was panting. He stopped, wiped the sweat from his forehead, then began walking again, dragging his suitcase, breathing heavily. Finally, Bennett flung open his front door and went out to his uncle, picked up his suitcase, and led him into the house.

Maury rarely traveled from his house, much less from the city of Memphis. He hugged Bennett happily, dropped his heavy alpaca coat on the floor, and sank into a chair.

Jesus, it's good to be here, he said, looking around the room. Could I have a Coca-Cola? He took off his hat. The bald spot of years past had now completely taken over his head, there was no point in trying to cover it, and both Maury's hands fidgeted uselessly in his lap.

Never been through Virginia and Maryland before, said Maury, still catching his breath. Pretty country. Near Bristol, the toilet got jammed. We had to stop every fifty miles until we could change buses in Washington. Maury tenderly rubbed his groin, as if remembering the strain on his bladder. He stretched his legs. With the Coke, he was slowly reviving.

The telephone rang. It was for Maury. He got a look of embarrassment and took the call in another room, with the door closed.

I'm sorry, he said softly, after returning. I only gave your number to one person. Maybe two. He sat back down in the embroidered wing chair without looking at Bennett and quietly sipped on his Coke.

It was only five in the afternoon but already getting dark. Bennett still hadn't gotten used to the long winters up north. He got up and turned on two lamps, then carefully closed the shades in his living room. He picked up a book lying on a table, returned it to the bookcase in the corner, and sat down on the sofa across from his uncle.

Haven't had a road trip in years, Maury said. Ever tell you about my trip to Miami in the '35 Ford? No, said Bennett. Maury laughed and kicked his suitcase, making a metallic rattle. I was in my second year at Vandy. Before the trouble. It was spring vacation. Had a good friend named G. L. Harrison. G. L. wore a raccoon coat year-round. He kept a bottle of Tennessee whiskey in one pocket and two packs of cigarettes in the other. Now, G. L. had come into the possession of a dark green

1935 Ford. It was a beauty. We're driving around Nashville one day during spring vacation and G.L. says it's getting a little boring. Nothing but bananas today, he used to say. So we decide to drive east and south. We just kept right on going and going and ended up driving clear down to Miami. We had nothing with us but the clothes on our back and a very limited amount of spending money. We hung out in Miami for five days. Slept in the car. First day, we met some slickers from Atlanta and lost the car in a card game. Then won it back from the same fellows a day later. Maury smiled. That second day at the table, we were really going to town, he said. We took in a little extra and decided we would just see the sights for the rest of the time. We get back to Nashville and G.L.'s girlfriend is waiting for us with her dad, asking about her car. Not to worry, says G.L., and he hands her the keys.

Maury took a long drink from his Coke. How's the teaching? Good, said Bennett. Maury nodded his head with satisfaction. You've been at, you've been at, what's the name? Leominster, said Bennett. Right, said Maury. Leominster. You've been at Leominster four or five years now, haven't you? Yes, said Bennett. Still haven't hooked up serious with a woman, huh? said Maury. No, Bennett said. You will, said Maury. You will. The women don't know what they're missing.

## Good Benito

What are you, twenty-eight, twenty-nine now? Thirty,
said Bennett. God, time goes by, said Maury. Time does
goes by. I guess Marty must be about twenty-seven,
then, and Philip twenty-five. What's Marty up to? He's
an accountant at Central Maine Power in Thurston,
near Portland, said Bennett. Four years now. You been
up there? asked Maury. No, said Bennett, Marty's invited me but I haven't been yet. I hear it's pretty country up there, said his uncle. I'm proud of you, Bennett.
Being a professor and all. You studied like hell. You deserve it. You're a good kid.

It was now completely dark outside. Maury
looked at his watch and his body straightened up. Mind
if I turn on the TV? he asked. *Marina* is on. It's already
too late for *One Day to Live.*

Go ahead, said Bennett, I'll take your suitcase to
your room. Bennett hefted the suitcase with a grunt
and realized that Maury hadn't mentioned the length
of his stay. He walked down the hall to the spare bedroom and put the suitcase in the closet. The room
smelled fresh from the clean sheets, and Bennett lin-
gered and looked at the photograph on the bureau,
himself and his two brothers at a graduation somewhere. He was glad that Maury had come.

How are things with you, Maury? Bennett asked
when he got back to the living room. All right, said

Maury, all right. He hesitated. Actually, he said, not so good. Your mother talk to you about me recently? No, said Bennett. Maury turned down the TV and sat down heavily on the sofa, next to Bennett. He let out a sigh. Your parents stopped paying the rent on West Galloway, he said, looking down at his hands. It was a wonderful thing they did for me all those years. His voice trembled. I guess they couldn't do it forever.

Why did they stop? asked Bennett. Maury sighed again. His eyes moistened. I guess I was an embarrassment to them. They wanted me out of east Memphis. You can't blame them.

Shit, said Bennett, I'm sorry. When did this happen? Six months ago, said Maury. Marlene is storing my things in her basement. Sweet Marlene.

Six months, said Bennett. Where have you been the last six months? I know someone in Germantown, said Maury. Moved in with him for two months. He really didn't have room. Then I slept in the immigrant dorm at B'nai B'rith for three months. They let people stay without paying, until they can find another place. Maury leaned his head back and looked at the ceiling. Bennett, he said, I'm almost sixty years old.

Bennett looked across the room, into the kitchen. He was thinking of the many times he had ridden his bike to Maury's house on Galloway, past the houses on Gwynne with the honeysuckle growing on the front fences. He was thinking about sitting with Maury on his couch. Telling Maury about Leila. Clothes piled on the boxes.

You could go to that place in Fraser, said Bennett. What's the name of that place? I don't remember the name. You might be able to stay there indefinitely. Maury nodded. I know the place, he said. I might end up there.

It might not be so bad, said Bennett. No, said Maury. I think I could live there. It'd be crowded. I'd have to give up my furniture and stuff. Not my tools. I'd rather live somewhere else, naturally, but I could live there. I might end up there.

Could you pay a little rent? asked Bennett. Maury shrugged his shoulders and didn't answer. Money, for Maury, was not a solid. It was a liquid, or a gas.

Could I have another Coke? asked Maury. Of course, said Bennett. Remember that time I fixed the stereo in your house? said Maury. Bennett smiled, remembering. Your mother was having one of her parties, Maury continued. She called me up special, just to come over and fix the stereo for the party. And we did it, didn't we? We got it. Maury chuckled.

I remember, said Bennett. You found a short in

the amplifier. You found it in ten minutes and sent me to the utility room to get some electrician's tape. Mother was in there, about to faint she was so nervous. She stayed there all afternoon until the stereo was fixed and the food was prepared. You were amazing, the way you found that short so fast.

Maury beamed. Your mother called me up special for that one, he said again. We got 'em, didn't we? We certainly did. Maury put on his Dodgers cap again and sat back in his chair, still smiling. Bennett was smiling too, lost in the memories.

Maybe the place in Fraser, said Maury, talking to himself. He got up and turned the television back up, returned to the couch and his Coke. They sat together, watching television.

A hot water pipe creaked. Immediately, Maury went to his room and came back with a handful of wrenches. I can fix that pipe, he said, talking over a woman on the television. I'd enjoy fixing it for you. It's not broken, said Bennett. It sounds like that when the heat first comes on. Sounds broken to me, said Maury, and he began moving tentatively toward the baseboard. Please, Uncle Maury, said Bennett, please don't. Maury hesitated. Then he nodded and sat down. You just let me know if anything needs fixing, he said and turned his attention back to the television.

.   .   .

That night Bennett had a dream. He was lecturing in front of his students, standing at the blackboard. He looked down and was shocked to discover that he wasn't wearing any pants. His students seemed to notice at the same time and smirked at his nakedness. Then he was in his living room. The room began spinning around, flooded with green and orange lights, humming. We can't stop it! someone yelled. Books began falling off the bookshelves onto the floor. It's not perpendicular! someone else yelled. The refrigerator door was wide open. Food was rotting. We can't stop it, we can't stop it. Miz Lang's fainted, Florida said. I'll get the smelling salts. The green and orange lights glared on the furniture, vibrated with the hum. The room continued to spin. Brown boxes were piled up everywhere, in the living room, in Bennett's study, in his bedroom. Dirty clothes lay on the tables. Uncle Maury came out of his room. He was living with Bennett. He sat down on the floor, looking contented and distant. The green and orange lights flickered on his bald head. Look what you've done, Bennett screamed at his uncle. Maury looked puzzled and defenseless. Rain began falling into the room, through the holes in the roof. Look what you've done, shouted Bennett again. The room spun faster and faster. Bennett was thrown to the floor. The humming was a yellow explosion in his ears. Florida came into the room, saw Bennett lying on the floor, and placed the smelling salts up to his nose.

Bennett stands with his uncle on the landing, waiting for the bus to depart. The air has the smell of gasoline exhaust and it is cold and people stand huddled in small groups. Never did get to use my tools, says Maury with a sad smile. Next time I come, I'm going to have to break something in your house so I can fix it. Maury's breath makes fleeting wisps in the cold winter air. He has on his alpaca coat and his Dodgers hat and a package of food under his arm. It did me good to visit you, Bennett, he says. A lot of good. He hugs his nephew. The sun shines cold and hard on the aluminum side of the station. Bennett strains to hold back his tears. He cannot bring himself to do what he knows he should do, perhaps what he wants to do. And now, the four days are over and he stands here with his uncle at this moment in the cold sun. He cannot talk. He has no words. The bus driver calls out that the bus is leaving. Maury hugs Bennett again, thanks him again. Bennett hugs his uncle back, hard, squeezes his shoulder and his hand, helps him up the first stair.

At the age of thirty-two, Bennett was promoted to full professor at Leominster. He was at the peak of his powers. His research was being referred to at the major international conferences, he had received job offers from Chicago and Princeton, he got weekly invitations from his old fellow graduate student, Ralph Jenkins, now head of the physics department at Stanford. Bennett couldn't sleep. But his sleeplessness was not from the excitement of success. He would wake up in the middle of the night feeling like he wanted to jump out of his skin, get out of bed and try to read, stare, fidgeting, at the blue metallic streetlamp outside his window. His skin seethed. His life was a 500-watt bulb inside a small black box. He was drying up inside, and his skin happened to be the first part to notice. He was not thinking of love. He just needed to soothe his skin and to sleep.

He pursued several women, but without satisfaction. He would sit in restaurants and talk to them and find himself unable to imagine touching them.

For three months, he dated a woman named Janet, a schoolteacher. She was smart and Bennett liked talking to her. I love you, Bennett, she said after the second month, but I can't see you both Saturday and Sunday. Saturday I take Mr. Pips for his lessons. Mr. Pips was Janet's Scottish terrier. Bennett looked at Janet with a baffled expression. Oh, sweetie, she said, I can see that you don't think I love you. Of course I do. I love you, Mr. Pips, my mother, and my house, in that order.

Janet showed Bennett how to double-tie his shoelaces, so that they would never come untied.

**B**ennett sat on a promontory over the Chesapeake, gazing at the water. He had been coming here for several months, ever since his trip to see Florida. When he'd heard she was dying, he had gone immediately to Memphis, then spent two days sitting in the living room of his parents' house with his face buried in his hands, unable to go to the hospital where she lay.

He sat above the bay and thought about nothing and felt the cool dark of the night. The night was exceedingly dark, and the water as still as a held breath, and as his eyes slowly adjusted to the black he saw something fantastic: diamonds shimmering on the water. Reflections of stars in the bay. Occasionally, a gentle ripple would sweep through the black carpet of water, perhaps made by a fish, and the stars slipped together, then apart.

He'd been sitting spellbound for an hour when he saw the roving beam of a flashlight. Then the voices of two women. They'd gotten lost and couldn't find the sandy path back to their car. He knew the way. The three of them walked together, single file, their footsteps making muffled thuds in the sand. They had all been hypnotized by the tiny points of light in the water and felt a silent union as they walked.

One of the women was Penny. When they got back to the cars, she and Bennett exchanged names and telephone numbers. They were not courting each other. Rather, they sensed that neither of them might ever see an evening like this again, that they were somehow connected, joined by this night. She scribbled her number quickly, in the small glow of the flashlight. He didn't see her face.

Two weeks later she called. She worked afternoons at a credit bureau in Washington. Would he like to meet her after work for a drink? Yes.

Penny needed him from the beginning, and that need drew him to her. She was twenty-five. Her parents were divorced. She was a painter. She painted in a studio until early afternoon, when the light began to shift, then went to her job at the credit bureau. She lived on very little.

They met the second time at an outdoor café called Tivoli, near Dupont Circle. The café had five enamel tables with white wrought-iron chairs and window boxes with petunias. There was a green door to the inside with a lot of brass on it and a sign saying Welcome Lucarno.

It was a humid evening in July. They were both perspiring heavily. Penny was blond, with a fine, soft down covering her body, and her perspiration shimmered on her face and the back of her neck. They sat at the one empty table, started with the dark night on the Chesapeake and went backwards from there.

She was fair-skinned and fragile, with light in her hair. She wore a sleeveless blouse, which revealed freckles against the white of her arms. And she had a sad, distant look in her eyes, even when she smiled.

They ordered lemonade. Penny never drank alcohol. Her mother was an alcoholic. So they drank lemonade. Bennett said that he had tried to memorize every detail of that night on the bay, the stillness, the feel of the air, the shape of the shore. She laughed and told him a story about Degas, who was a firm believer in memory drawing. In Degas's ideal painting school, the first-year students would set up their easels on the first floor, where the model posed. The second-year students had their easels on the second floor, the third-year students on the third. The second- and third-year students would have to run down the stairs, study the model, then run back up the stairs and paint what they had seen. The more advanced the student, the longer he would be required to remember his last glimpse of the model. She laughed again. Her laugh was musical. She told stories about other painters, Tarbell and Sargent and Cassatt, as if she had worked in their studios. The hours disappeared. They forgot about dinner.

He noticed that she rarely looked at him. She looked at her lemonade glass, or at her sketchbook on the table, or off down the street. Even when she talked to him, she didn't hold his eyes. However, he looked at her, and he thought that he had never seen so lovely a woman in his life.

She happened to mention that she had come to the café by the subway. Her car was in the shop and needed a new transmission. It would be expensive. He startled both of them by offering to lend her the money. The words just rushed out. After an awkward silence, she thanked him but said she would work it out.

Around eleven, she said that she needed to go home. She let him walk her to the subway stop.

They began calling each other in the evenings. She hated her job at the credit bureau. She had low status there because she worked only half-days. She was paid minimum wage and treated with contempt. But it was the only part-time job she could find. She had to have the mornings to paint.

She had painted since childhood. At the age of seventeen, during her last year of high school, she ran away from home, from Pittsburgh, landed in Washington, and met Jeremy Gaunt. Gaunt was a master painter who had been trained in the classical tradition, and he taught in the classical tradition. She had been painting in his atelier for seven years. Gaunt ministered to about a dozen students. Many of them were now so accomplished that they exhibited their own paintings and sold them at good prices.

Bennett began taking off mornings to watch Penny paint, leaving Baltimore at dawn, coming back at noon for his classes. The studio was on a busy street in Silver Spring, a large airy room with twenty-foot ceilings and huge north-facing windows. It was an old building with creaking floorboards. Charcoal dust and the odor of turpentine filled the air. Vases, dried flowers, small porcelain figures, coins, folded fabrics lay scattered about, bric-a-brac for still lifes. He sat in a chair in the back of the room, breathing in the turpentine air and watching Penny and the others work. He watched the way she studied her subject, the way she selected her colors and frowned, the way that she tilted her head. He wanted to know everything about her. In the middle of the morning, she took a break, would walk back to his chair and smile at him, without saying anything. They would leave the studio and walk slowly down the creaking hallway, past the old hand-opened elevator. On Tuesdays and Fridays, Gaunt appeared to give critiques. A short, bearded man of about fifty, Gaunt would walk up to each easel, say a few words, then walk to another, the apprentices straining to catch every word.

After a month, Bennett saw one of Penny's portraits. It was an exquisite pastel picture of a little girl holding a doll. The child had moist eyes, as if she'd been crying, but at the same time seemed like she was stifling a smile. She was alive. The painting had been neglected. Its edges were beginning to curl and the pastel to smear. Can I frame it? Bennett asked. What for? Penny answered and dropped it behind a radiator with her other paintings. She never framed or exhibited her work.

Some evenings, they met at restaurants. Their favorite was an underground place in Georgetown. It had three small rooms, each lined with bookshelves, like a private library. The walls were brick and cool and gave a red tint to the air in the candlelight. They would sit at one of the wood tables and have fruit juice and order dinner and talk about painting. One night he wanted her to draw something for him. She protested that the light wasn't steady, and he kept asking her, and finally she said she would like to draw a portrait of him. He moved to the other side of the table and sat very still, and she began to draw his head and his shoulders. It was the first time she had looked directly at him. She used a sketching pencil and worked very slowly, and the shadows jumped around in the flickering light, but she waited patiently for the periods of even light and kept working. After an hour she began to get a fine likeness. People came over from another table to watch. Immediately, she closed her sketch pad and put it back in her bag. The people whispered something to themselves and went back to their table. I'm sorry, she said softly, I don't like to be stared at. He smiled at her and held her hand and she looked beautiful in the candlelight. Tell me about your work, she said. Tell me, really. He began explaining the details of his research. She listened for a few minutes and then said, You're doing something important, Bennett. He knew that she didn't understand what he was talking about, but he believed her.

He invited her to Baltimore. Oh no, I couldn't do that, she said, shaking her head and looking down at the table. But she began letting him drive her home, to her apartment on Lamont Street, near the navy yard. He never went in. They would sit in his car outside the apartment for an hour and watch the wavering of a streetlamp, masked and unmasked by the leaves of a tree, and she would lean her head back in the crook of his arm. Sometimes they would turn on the radio, very low, and listen to jazz. It would be ten or eleven at night.

One night very late, when Bennett couldn't sleep, he called her. It was two in the morning. He had to see her, he said. She said something sleepily, and he got in his car and drove to her apartment. He didn't wait at the red lights. When he walked in, she was wearing a white cotton robe. She whispered that they had to be quiet, her roommate was sleeping. They sat on the couch. She started to cry. Just hold me, she said softly. I can't stand it any longer, he said. I know, she replied. They sat for a while without talking, just holding each other. Then she took his hand and led him into her bedroom. The next morning, she allowed him to give her the $200 she needed to release her car from the repair shop.

## Good Benito

They went for a drive in her resuscitated car. They didn't care where they were going. They just drove, alighting at random places. It was a warm day in September. They rode with the windows down. In mid-afternoon they found themselves following a small road west of Washington. The sun was angling across a tall field of grass and a light wind was blowing, stirring up little whirlpools of dust on the road. They parked her car by the side of the road and wandered across the field. After about a quarter of a mile, from the top of a ridge they spotted an abandoned railroad car, sitting by itself in the grass. Strangely, no tracks were in sight, as if the car had been dropped from the sky. They raced down the hill and climbed into the car through one of its open doors. It had evidently been a freight car. Sacks of flour stood in the corners. They were alone and it was cool inside the car and the sun threw shafts of light on the soft wooden floor. They stood there in the cool, and without saying a word she took off her clothes and rubbed flour all over her body. Then she did the same to him. The flour felt cool on their bare skin. The flour floated in the air, caught in the sunlight slanting through the car, turning the air white. They made love leaning against the wall. Afterwards, as they stood there naked and white, still locked to each other, she wiped the flour from his nose and whispered, I don't deserve you. How can you say that? he said. Don't ever leave me, she said, looking directly into his eyes. I won't ever leave you, he said. He didn't want her to leave him either, but he never told her so.

She knew the richest gardens in Maryland and took him there, taught him to see beauty in even common flowers—the delicate white wisps of baby's breath, the soft red centers of China pinks, the layered puffs of portulaca. She knew the songs and the colorings of birds and taught him the white-crowned sparrow, the sanderling, the phoebe, the nuthatch. She knew every indentation of the Chesapeake.

She told him that outside, shadows have cool colors and lights have warm colors, while inside, shadows have warm colors and lights cool. He told her that bubbles are spheres because a spherical shape minimizes surface area for a given volume. She told him that sea anemones and hermit crabs live in a harmony; the anemones hide the crabs from their enemies, while the crabs carry the anemones on their backs to new feeding grounds. He told her that gravity has the elegant property that it accelerates all objects equally; thus astronauts orbit the earth on precisely the same trajectory as their spaceship and float within it.

When she woke him at dawn by lightly sweeping her nipples across his back, he sometimes forgot who he was.

Two years after they were married, Branscombe, the most prestigious art gallery in Washington, had a show of contemporary classical realism and invited Penny to exhibit her paintings, alongside those of several other leading artists in the area. Gaunt had recommended Penny's work. The gallery director had visited Gaunt's studio one day when Penny wasn't there and privately viewed the paintings behind the radiator.

Bennett was sitting on the sofa in the living room when he first read the admiring letter from the director. He threw down the other mail and began crowing. Penny had been rejecting his compliments for several years, but here was a compliment she couldn't ignore.

And, for the first time, her work would be publicly recognized. People came down from New York to see the openings at Branscombe.

I'm not doing it, Penny said quietly. What are you talking about? Bennett shouted in disbelief. I'm not doing it, she repeated. They're showing Kresky and Ingbretson. So what? he said. I'm not in that league, she replied. What do you call this? Bennett said, waving the letter. Lippmann has seen your work. He says you're in that league. She went back to her art magazine. Dammit, Penny, Bennett yelled, the first time he had yelled at her. This is your chance. What have you been doing for the last fifteen years? I've been learning to paint, she answered.

They went to the opening. Penny didn't even introduce herself to Mr. Lippmann as he circled through the crowd shaking hands. Bennett was so angry that he couldn't look at the paintings of Kresky and Ingbretson. He sat in a chair for the evening, holding a half-glass of pink wine.

Perhaps if he hadn't pushed her, things might have been different. What right did he have to be ambitious for her? He shouldn't have pushed her.

No, thinking back on it later, it wasn't his ambition. It was Penny. She had no confidence in the future. She often said that she couldn't believe she was married, as if she had given herself to the past, to being alone for her life. She wouldn't quit her dreadful job at the credit union, even though he pleaded with her to leave it, to devote herself completely to painting. He was earning enough for them both. But she wouldn't do it. She didn't trust the future.

She was afraid that she would turn into her mother, who arrived on a bus once or twice a year, without any notice, and stayed with them a few days. Penny's mother had carelessly dyed hair and a wild, bloodshot look in her eyes, but you could see that she once had been beautiful. Bennett would find her sitting on the front steps when he got home. He would tell her when Penny was due and help her to the extra bedroom. She was always exhausted when she first arrived and would collapse on her bed without taking off her clothes and sleep through the night. The next morning, Penny would begin crying, half in joy over being near the one person she loved besides Bennett, half in sorrow at her mother's disintegrating condition. She would scold her mother about her shoddy clothes, and why didn't she cash the check Penny had sent her. Then they would hug and kiss, and Penny would make her mother a big breakfast and take her to the doctor's.

That night, she and her mother would have a terrible fight in the living room about her mother's drinking. Finally, Penny would come to bed in tears. A half-hour later, lying in bed in the dark, they would hear the liquor cabinet quietly open. Penny begged her mother to come live with them, but her mother always refused.

Penny carried with her everywhere a small, blue brocaded purse containing fifty dollars. Bennett never saw her without it. At night, she put it on the table beside her bed. What's that for? he asked her once. Just in case, she answered, and wouldn't say anything more. As if a flood might come in the night, washing her far away from him, from everyone who could help her. As if she expected that any day she might get fired from her job, come home, find that he had deserted her and left nothing.

Even when she was outdoors, which she adored, he could sense her feeling of hopelessness. She would smile for a moment, lost in the picture before her, and then that sad, distant look returned to her eyes. That look became Bennett's enemy. What was she thinking about? Her wretched childhood? Her poor mother? The imaginary life in the magazines?

.  .  .

They sat in the living room, in dim light, after Bennett had finished the dishes. She was reading her art magazine, reading by the light from the kitchen. I still haven't learned how to get the big look, she said, sighing. I've been with Gaunt eleven years. Bennett was silent. After several years of contradicting her when she bemoaned her slow progress in the studio, he was now silent.

Let's dance, she said. She went to the cabinet and pulled out an old record, one that she'd listened to as a girl, and put down the needle on Someone to Watch Over Me. They began moving around the room very slowly, her head turned away from his, her eyes closed. I'm not losing the edges, she said. My pictures look like number paintings. He was silent. They moved slowly around the room, passing the sofa, the table with the carved boxes, the embroidered wing chair. There's a somebody I'm longing to see, I hope that he, turns out to be, someone to watch over me, Penny sang softly along with the record. They moved in languid circles. The roomed brightened for a moment as a car came down the street, its headlights sweeping the curtains. Then the half-darkness again, the shadows of cobalt. Bennett felt as if he were watching himself from a corner of the room, watching the two of them. He said nothing, he just watched as his life happened, angled through glass to this room and this moment. The song finished, but they kept dancing. They kept dancing as if still hearing music, circling slowly past the sofa, the table with carved boxes, the embroidered chair. All of which he saw from his other place in the corner. They kept moving, slowly and without words.

That night, as she undressed before bed, he didn't remark on her beauty. She always denied what he said of her beauty. That night he said nothing.

He began helping her tear herself down. He would point out that such and such a person in her studio was showing his work at some gallery. She would nod her head silently. He would make references to books that he knew she hadn't read. One Sunday afternoon, while she was in the bathroom, he hid her blue brocaded purse under the mattress in the spare bedroom. She noticed it was gone and she panicked and flew through the house looking for it. My God, she repeated, turning over pillows, opening drawers, slamming them shut. My God. What's the matter, Pen? he said. I've lost it, she said, terrified, and continued to search. After a half-hour he returned the purse to the kitchen table, where she had left it.

He was vicious. What little dignity she had, he destroyed. He despised himself for the way he began treating her but was astonished to find that he had no control of his actions. He couldn't understand how he could have no control of himself. Minutes after he'd said something cruel, he would go outside and slam his hand against the brick front of the house, hoping the pain would give him control. But the next day, it would happen all over again.

In the last year of their marriage, he stayed many nights at the college, working late. He did long and tedious calculations. Those calculations saved him from himself. When he would get home, she was usually up, waiting. She had made extra dinner and sat with him while he ate. Afterwards, they would walk from room to room turning off lights, until the house was as dark as that first night on the Chesapeake. Then they would go to bed, without saying a word.

One evening, as he sat in his office, something changed in his mind. He suddenly felt he had regained control. He had been acting illogically. He had a problem, like any other problem. The problem just hadn't been well posed. The problem was: Should he leave Penny or not? He began reviewing their relationship, listing the pros and the cons, which became zigzags of a curve in his mind, a curve arcing to some definite conclusion. A wave of relief swept over him.

When he arrived home that night the house was dark. She had not waited up for him. He sat in a chair in the living room and resumed analyzing the curve in his mind. He turned on a single lamp, and the air glowed in a dim, yellow light. He must have been pondering in that low yellow light for a long time when he felt a hand on his shoulder. What time is it? she said. He looked at his watch. Midnight. She stared at him oddly. What's the matter, Bennett? she asked. Nothing, he said. You're crying, she said. He put his hand to his face, and he found it was wet. I'm all right, he said. Let's go to bed.

The next day, he told her he wanted a separation. She didn't ask why. She didn't argue. He insisted that she stay in the house. He rented a small apartment for himself several miles away and moved out, in the middle of the night so that their neighbors wouldn't notice.

He sent her weekly checks, more than she needed. She began calling him at the college. How are you? she'd say. I'm all right, he'd answer. When will we see each other? she'd ask. I don't know, he'd say. You left your blue denim coat, she said once. I don't need it, he answered.

Bennett didn't tell anyone at Leominster about

the separation. He was too embarrassed. He didn't know anyone well. He called his mother. She waited a while before replying and then said, We knew that something like this would happen. She paused again, as if thinking, then said, Your father and I would be grateful if you could wait a few days before telling anyone else in Memphis. I'm sorry for you, Bennett.

He sent John a letter. He hadn't seen John for nearly twenty years, and he knew John wouldn't answer, but he wanted him to know.


One night, a month after the separation had begun, he was walking to his new apartment, nearing the front door, when she suddenly appeared from behind a hedge near the entrance. She'd been waiting for him. She began weeping. Bennett, she said, come back. I'll do whatever you want. Please, please come back. I can't, he said. Bennett, please, she said. She threw her arms around his waist and held on as he tried to open the door. Please, Bennett, she said. Please come back to me. I can't, he said again. She was still holding on to him. He pulled her arms away, struggled with her, pushed himself inside the door and quickly closed it. He realized he was sobbing. His temples were pounding. He vomited. He crawled to the bathroom.

A week later, in the middle of the night, he was awakened by the ringing of the telephone. It was her. How are you, Bennett? she said. Jesus, Penny, it's two in the morning, he said. I've swallowed twenty sleeping pills, she said.

When he got to the house, ten minutes later, she was lying across the bed in her nightgown. That bedroom, that space he had shared with her, seemed like a compartment in an alien spaceship. A rug, tables, a chair, all unrecognizable. She lifted her head slightly when he walked in. Hi, Bennett, she said. Her head fell back down heavily on the bed. He grabbed the empty bottle beside her, threw a robe around her, carried her to his car.

The regional hospital was fifteen minutes away. By the time they got there, she was unconscious. Her face had lost color. Bennett flew into the emergency room, carrying Penny in his arms. She was weightless. The nurse who'd been sitting at the triage desk ran over when she saw him burst through the double doors. What happened? she said. He handed her the empty bottle. The nurse read the label quickly, then bent down to see if Penny was breathing. She put her fingers on Penny's wrist. Her pulse is weak, she said. How many did she take? She told me twenty, Bennett said. My God, said the nurse. When? I don't know, he said, maybe an hour ago. Let's hope, said the nurse. By then, they'd maneuvered Penny to a wheelchair, where she slumped with her head hanging down to one side and dribble coming out of her mouth. The triage nurse wheeled her away, shouting for Nurse Burson.

Things began to happen very very slowly, as if the entire emergency ward were deep under water, at the bottom of a swimming pool. While the triage nurse was moving down the hall with Penny, shouting for the other nurse, Bennett noticed two people sitting in chairs in the waiting room. One was a woman with a checkered dish towel wrapped around her hand. The other was a young blond-haired man in a long leather coat. They were frozen, they were statues. Bennett noticed that a television was on, mounted high on the wall of the waiting room. Some late-night movie was playing; the people were talking sluggishly, so that Bennett could hear long spaces between each word. He looked off in the direction of the nurse. She was running in slow motion, her legs caught in the thick liquid of the underwater room. He looked down and saw the linoleum floor, looked at its tiles, stretching tile by tile by tile from him to them. Then Bennett noticed that he too was running, but in slow motion, running after his wife, who was slumped unconscious in a wheelchair with the white of the nurses all around her. His eyes inched upward along his legs to his arms, and he saw for the first time that he was carrying Penny's socks.

The nurses went past the barracks room with the rows of beds and movable curtains and wheeled Penny down the hall to a private room. When Bennett arrived there, an unmeasurable time later, she was stretched out on a bed with her head propped up high. A nurse was feeding a plastic tube down Penny's throat, very very slowly. Every now and then, she would squeeze a bulb, forcing air down the tube, put her ear against Penny's chest listening intently, then push the tube further. It's in her stomach, she said finally, and slowly. Then she pumped water down the tube. Eventually, some ugly brown liquid with lumps gurgled back up the tube. This was directed into a pot. Meanwhile, one of the nurses had hooked up an I.V. to Penny's arm. She came over to Bennett, where he was sitting on a chair by the bed, and said, It's good you got her here in time. Her words were distant rustles of leaves. He was absently studying the delicate veins just under the skin of Penny's arm. The charcoal now, said a nurse. Then she turned to Bennett and said, The charcoal absorbs what's left in her stomach. It's good you got her here in time. It's good you were so calm.

He was sitting there when she awakened, a few hours later. He had been gazing at a clock on the wall, watching its second hand creep around the face. Dawn light was just seeping in through the windows. She opened her eyes and looked at him and smiled weakly. Hi, Bennett, she said softly. She held out her hand, and he took it, holding her hand in his hand. Wouldn't it be nice to have the Halleys over, she said, now that you're back. He said nothing. She gave him a long look, then turned her head and went back to sleep.

**K**atie shrieks as she makes out a seal fifty yards away. Look, Uncle Bennett, she shouts and points from the bow. Look. I saw his whiskers. She begins paddling furiously, banging the side of the canoe and splashing water everywhere. I want to touch him, she says. The seal pokes his head above water, looks around, lazily does a somersault, and then sinks below the dark glass of sea. He's gone, says Bennett. We should have invited him for dinner. Seals don't come in the house, says the little girl.

They are rounding a small island. Some distance away, a cormorant plows through the water, fiercely flaps its wings, struggles to become airborne. It eventually succeeds and noiselessly joins a flock overhead. Some seagulls fly by, squawking loudly. Low tide. Rocks usually submerged peer above the surface for their brief hour of air, tiny islands, each with its own headdress of gold sea kelp, attached shells, visiting gulls. Docks off the mainland float close to the bottom. Some are beached, their boats grounded and tilted at odd angles.

Bennett lays down his paddle. For the moment, the tidal current has ceased, the canoe drifts in still water. He trains his binoculars on the island. He can see a single house, gray cedar shingles, a brick chimney, white posts on a porch, cathedral windows. Spruce trees grow thickly, march down to the shore, to the oblong angled rocks. He spots a great nest high in one tree. A mother osprey sits there, her eyes riveted on the canoe. Here, Katie, have a look, Bennett says. He passes the binoculars to his niece, touches her on the shoulder. Over there, he says, and points at the osprey's nest. I can't see it, wails Katie, I can't see it. There, Bennett says. There. I see it, she says. How many ospreys live there? I don't know, says Bennett, but it's a big nest. He holds out his thumb at arm's length and sizes the nest, then does the same to the house, comparing their angular widths. It's bigger than the nest on Orr's Island, he says. You remember the one we saw yesterday on Orr's Island? Yesss, she says, dragging out the *s* in a long, fancy hiss.

## Good Benito

Hundreds of lobster buoys glitter in the water. Reds, greens, blues, lavenders. They dance back and forth with each passing wave. Just now, a boat motors up to a buoy near the canoe. A lobsterman in a bright orange slicker cranks in the rope on the float, hauls up the trap. He takes out two lobsters, measures them with his calipers, keeps one and tosses the other overboard, rebaits the trap, and drops it back in the ocean. Here we are in the big city, turkey toes, WDIX Portland, blares the radio on his control console. Bennett waves hello. The lobsterman nods, spins his boat gracefully with the small triangular sail in the stern and motors to his next trap.

Do you live in Japan? asks Katie. No, says Bennett, I live in Maryland. I live in Maine, says the child. Yes, you do, says Bennett, smiling. Why don't you ever come to our house? she asks. Bennett looks away, to the far shore, then back to Katie. I'm going to start coming, he says, I promise. I can swim, she says. Can I get in the water and show you? Let's wait until we're back in shallow water, he says. I want to fish, shouts Katie. It's too late to fish, says Bennett. It's after six. You promised, bawls the little girl. Daddy said you would take me fishing and you promised. Yes, I did, says Bennett and smiles. Oh, goodie, says Katie. She looks back at her uncle and grins, a large gap in her top front teeth. She has the bluest eyes of any child in the world. They are the deep blue of the sky. Sky blue.

Don't turn the handle, says Bennett. Just hold on with both hands and let the line drag in the water. I'll paddle. Will the fish know where to come? asks Katie. They'll know, he says. Can we stay out all night? asks Katie. We can sleep in the canoe. Your mother is making dinner, says Bennett. We have to go home for dinner.

The air thickens, becomes milky, diaphanous. A fog moves in, taking its time. In the distance, the main-land grows fuzzy and blurred. Colors fade first, leaving blue tones and grays, foggy shapes. Then these too melt away, into white. Closer by, other things slowly merge with the mist—the south point of the island, the brass bell on the channel marker, the archipelago of low-tide rocks. The Boston whaler moored off the east point turns gauzy and white, its gunnels grow cotton, its engine turns to a strange mound of snow, it fades and is gone. Lobster buoys dissolve one by one, the most distant first, then nearer and nearer, in decreasing circles. The air slowly grows thicker, opaline. The brittle threads of the osprey nest soften, merge with the trees, which themselves fuse and fade. And finally, the entire island, the last land on earth, slips into chalky oblivion.

What's happened? Where are we, Uncle Bennett?

asks Katie, excitedly. I don't know, says Bennett, I think I'll fish too. He gets out his pole. Will the fish still know where we are? asks the child with the sky eyes. Yep, says Bennett, fish like fog. The world around the canoe has dwindled in size to a translucent sphere several canoe lengths in diameter. The new world is a round dollop of water and air.

Is fog snow? asks Katie. No, says Bennett. It doesn't snow in the summer. Fog is like steam. It's a cloud that has dropped to the ground. Bennett puts down his fishing pole and looks out at the strange shrunken world, the small translucent sphere.

His eyes reach the edge of that sphere, an opaque, chalky wall. Then he imagines the invisible universe beyond. He imagines the small island with the single house, the wild raspberry brambles that spring up where trees fall, the spongy moss that grows in the shade. He hears the soft applause of poplars as their leaves flutter in wind, hears the chatter of red squirrels. He imagines the sun glinting off water in clear air, the liquid surface incandescent, shining, sparkling, quivering. He imagines the big boats going out for tuna, trailing their V-shaped wakes that jostle docks on the shore. Cormorants stretched out to dry on the rocks near the cove. The lobster marina near the east point, the bubbling storage pool filled with lobsters, the wooden traps stacked up like Coca-Cola crates, the pier, the steep ramp angling down to the float, the lobster boats tied to their moorings. He imagines the little road running from the marina, winding up the hill, past tidal inlets, past a string of cottages and mail boxes and tiny grocery stores, winding until it meets the highway and then north up to Thurston. In an aerial view, he looks down on the town, sees a green rectangle along the main street with the pagoda for summer concerts, the scattered roofs of the houses, the green-brown ribbon of a river, the crossing of railroad tracks. He sails high through the air, northward, along the coast to the delicate white of a beach, looks down at the tidal pools where children splash and play. He sees. He takes his last letter from John, many years old, and fashions it into a pair of wings. Looking up, he sees the blue of the sky, stretching higher and higher, growing thin with the diminishing density of air, turning pale and then dark.

Have you caught any fish yet, Uncle Bennett? she asks. Not yet, he says, have you? I don't think the fish know we're here, she says. Maybe you're right, he says and winks at her. Oh, Uncle Bennett, says Katie, and she giggles. Her laughter slips through the fog, bounces off the invisible coast, returns in a flight of high notes, fragile and flutelike.

## About the Author

**Alan Lightman** was born in Memphis, Tennessee, in 1948 and was educated at Princeton and at the California Institute of Technology. He has written for *Granta*, *Harper's*, *The New Yorker*, and *The New York Review of Books*. His previous books include *Time Travel and Papa Joe's Pipe*, *A Modern-Day Yankee in a Connecticut Court*, *Origins*, *Ancient Light*, *Great Ideas in Physics*, and *Time for the Stars*. *Einstein's Dreams* was his first book of fiction. He is professor of science and writing at the Massachusetts Institute of Technology.